Shamus

DEATH
OF
AN
ALASKAN
PRINCESS

1994

DEATH
OF
AN
ALASKAN
PRINCESS

*For Shamus, former
Juneauite —
Hope we see
you again!*

Bridget A. Smith

Bridget A. Smith

(206) 299-8117

2612 17th Alaska

Shamus

A
Joan
Kahn
BOOK

ST. MARTIN'S PRESS
NEW YORK

Copyeditor: Johanna Tani

LIBRARY OF CONGRESS
Library of Congress Cataloging-in-Publication Data

Smith, Bridget A.
Death of an Alaskan princess/by Bridget A. Smith.
p. cm.
ISBN 0-312-01336-1 : $12.95
I. Title.
PS3569.M5117D4 1988
813'.54—dc 19   87-29919
CIP

First Edition

10 9 8 7 6 5 4 3 2 1

To my husband, for his gift of time

DEATH
OF
AN
ALASKAN
PRINCESS

CHAPTER 1

E ven if Tyler hadn't telephoned me in desperation, any
opening of his protégé, David Whitmore, attracted
me like a salmon to herring eggs. Until a year ago,
David's paintings ranked as ordinary, best described as ro-
mantic Alaskana. Even though his work soared above the
painted gold pans that proliferate in gift-shop windows, it
still celebrated the wild in a sickly sentimental style. His
Dall sheep always stared balefully at distant enemies, his
bears always scooped red salmon out of streams with ferocity, his caribou always locked horns in combat. Strong
brushwork and true colors demonstrated his skill, but his
choice of subject and composition invariably disappointed
with their banality.

To his credit, David knew what his market craved: indi-
genous Alaskan life. At least he didn't romanticize the

Natives in the same way by painting Tlingit Indians dancing with knees bent, or Eskimos tossing someone in a blanket, or fat-cheeked Native children berry-picking. Hundreds of other artists covered that, thank you.

I prefer wild animals painted by artists who observe their subjects in their own habitats. In Southeastern Alaska, wild animals share the human habitat, but most humans rarely venture out into that of the animals. I suspect that David relied on *Alaska Magazine* photographs for inspiration. Or perhaps he watched eagles wheeling over the town or the bears foraging in garbage cans in the spring or the occasional seal who ventured into the harbor.

Then, a year ago, he climbed out of the rut of painting wild animals. I've known other artists who have changed their focus with incredible results. It freed David. I remember the first time I saw his new work at an opening at Tyler's gallery. Tyler dragged me by the hand to a painting in the corner. Bristling with power, a Raven, executed in the timeless style of the Northwest Coast Indians, but with its head studded with electronic circuitry, glared at me. "I'll take it," I whispered, hoping that no one else wanted it. Tyler chuckled, noticing my furtiveness. "He's trying out this new style. He doesn't think anyone will like it. I told him it's the best thing he's ever done." In Tlingit mythology, Raven created the world and is the star of many of the oral legends passed down from one generation to the next. The Raven and Eagle moieties form the foundation for the Tlingit clan system. In the "Electronic Raven," as David titled it, the inevitable collision of traditional Tlingit culture and western culture came to life.

Now that he has been discovered, I knew that I didn't

have to rush to David's show. I couldn't afford any of it now. Nothing of his sells for less than fifteen hundred dollars. The "Electronic Raven" is the only piece of his I own, and that I bought for one fifty. I do understand that painters have to eat, too, but the fees of a psychologist in private practice prevent me from playing hardball in the art world. I rely on Tyler to clue me in about new painters. Once they're established, they're out of my league.

Tyler's gallery lies only a few blocks away, as close to my office as every other building in downtown Juneau. The town rests against a narrow lip of land at the base of two mountains that plunge down to the sea. I breathed deeply of the air that promised spring, a bit dank, redolent of the moist earth feeling the sun for the first time in months. The fiddlehead ferns, still covered with papery brown wisps, were emerging. They reminded me of people in pain, tightly curled into a fist, holding their secrets in a hard pale green ball, defying anyone or anything to expose them to light. Nature prevails, of course, with people and with plants. It always does.

I didn't hurry to the gallery even though Tyler's voice had throbbed with emotion, a rare enough phenomenon for him. "Wynne, I know it is not good form to accost you in social situations, but I have to talk to you. I can't wait to make an appointment during office hours. I promise I'll make it up to you, maybe a discount on a piece." I knew then that whatever it was that he wanted to discuss was important; the offer of a discount on a painting was unprecedented. Tyler is not greedy, but he discovered how very difficult running a profitable art gallery can be. Fifteen years ago he stepped off the Alaska state ferry that runs from Seattle after a dismal three years in New York City as an aspiring artist with talent, but no training, with determination, but no experience in facing grueling competition. He elected to make his last stand in Juneau, swearing never to return to the small southern town where his genteel but poor family had lived "forever, my dear." Instead of painting, he nurtured other artists, lent them money, put them up in his tiny apartment, paid astronomical bar bills, arbitrated disputes. In return, he expected exclusive rights to the artists' work. Some balked. But Tyler kept them on a short leash. It seemed to me to be a tough way to get a return on an investment. With David, all of his work seemed to be paying off.

I pushed down my antagonistic feelings about David. Thank God, he wasn't a client of mine. For anyone to grow in therapy, a mutual feeling of positive regard has to exist. David's arrogance made me clench my teeth, maybe to prevent hostility from spilling out of my mouth. I resolved to relax, keep my thoughts to myself, and ignore anything stupid he said. I lifted my eyes to the spruce trees on the mountain pricking the sky, concentrating on the contrast of the blue-green with the pearl-gray. I heard a raven crying. No wonder the Indians credit them with supernatural powers. Sometimes they sound mournfully human.

I walked through the cream-colored door with the heavy brass hardware and groped my way up the dimly lit staircase. Nothing in Juneau can be reached easily. One either struggles up stairs or trips down stairs. A rush of warm moist air enveloped me as I walked through into the main gallery space. I touched the pearls around my neck. Jake had given them to me after an unusually successful fishing season. Since his death, the necklace had become a talisman. Tyler glided out of the crowd and took my hand.

"I wish I could paint you, Wynne. That blue matches your eyes. You look stunning."

"You're sweet, Tyler. You must be selling gobs."

"You know me too well. Every lawyer in town is here and they all seem to have pockets lined with money. I am in heaven."

"You're taking David straight to the top. Personality aside, I guess he deserves it."

"Naughty, naughty, Wynne. You mustn't be judgmental. Cardinal rule for clinical psychologists."

"Am I ever off duty?"

He shook his head. "No. Particularly not tonight. I need you." He looked over his shoulder, appraising the crowd. "I am sorry, Wynne, but I do need you."

"Right now?"

"It can wait until you've had your champagne and circulated."

"Who's here?"

"Everybody. The lawyers are rubbing tweedy shoulders, talking about paintings as investments. They just cannot buy anything for pleasure. The artists are in corners trying to figure out how to talk David into a trade. The state workers came after work, absolutely ravenous, and ate my centerpiece. The caterer was livid when she saw the damage. The legislators are self-medicating with enormous amounts of my champagne. David is surrounded by his coterie, expounding on *art* or some such nonsense." Tyler turned back to me with a sheen of tears over his bulging blue eyes. "I know it's awful cheek to want your advice outside of the office, Wynne, but I am desperate."

I muttered something soothing and watched him slip back into the crowd, his slender back held military-straight, his sandy hair thinning.

Heading for the champagne required considerable side-stepping accompanied by "pardon mes" through the crowd. The atmostphere was almost steamy. The smell of wet wool and Joy perfume mixed with a faint whiff of oil paints. I didn't really enjoy these things anymore. Not since the oil began flowing through the pipeline. One observant legislator, in a fit of honesty, said it turned us into sharks in a feeding frenzy. Greed triumphant. Instead of buying art for enjoyment, people talked about art as an investment, another commodity to be traded and used for a step up. At least Tyler benefited. His gallery occupies the second floor of a Victorian relic dating from the 1880s, when gold-crazed white men first settled in Juneau. Surprisingly, no fire ever swept through the original wooden buildings built on pilings on the beach. Now all piously preserved, the history of the town can be discerned by the careful observer—narrow streets intended for horses, the absence of right angles as the town grew organically around and up the mountains, the predominance of wood as a construction material giving way to a few buildings built in the thirties of stone when it looked as if it would be a permanent community. At different times the now airy gallery space housed a cigar factory, a saloon, a bordello, a drugstore, and a newspaper office. Fifteen-foot ceilings covered with the original stamped tin meet the walls in a fanciful swirl of plaster molding. Every surface is painted white, slightly different shades to enhance original features. Antique brass fixtures highlight the paintings. A thick room-size Chinese rug in cool greens covers the highly polished hardwood floor. I aimed for the small room through the wide arched doorway where Tyler traditionally set up a linen-draped table with champagne and hors d'oeuvres. Before I reached it, David hailed me.

"What do you think, Wynne?" He opened his arms wide.

His stance displayed his dreadful showmanship: a smocked white shirt with sash, green velvet trousers, and wooden clogs. In one ear hung a silver earring engraved with a stylized Eagle, symbol of a Tlingit moiety, one of the two basic tribal subdivisions, the other one being Raven. I debated about commenting on the outfit rather than the show but squelched the impulse. "I haven't been able to fight the crowd to get a closer look, David, but if it is totemic, I'll love it. My 'Electronic Raven' still thrills me after a year."

Magdalena spoke in surprise. "I didn't know that you were the one who bought it, Wynne."

David held his Tlingit companion tightly. "I am very grateful to Magdalena for teaching me about her heritage. The Northwest Coast Indians are fascinating to me." The warmth of David's voice and his obvious affection for Magdalena made me wonder for a few seconds if I wasn't too hard on him. Magdalena looked stunning as she leaned against David, smiling up at him. I noticed that her very dark eyes scanned the environment when they weren't prettily poised on her boyfried. Like a huntress deeply aware of her surroundings, she appeared relaxed, yet I knew she was noticing every detail. Her thick black hair swung free of her shoulders in a pageboy, unlike many Tlingit women, who allow it to grow down their backs into a point. Each time she moved her head to smile at me, at David, and to gaze around her, the tiny beads on her porcupine-quill earrings glittered.

David couldn't allow much silence. He took the floor again. "Did you know, Wynne, that in addition to being the Creator of the world, Raven is also a Trickster?" My warm feeling for him evaporated. He was beginning a lecture on Tlingit culture. I looked around wildly for release. It came from an unexpected source.

I heard a deep, unfamiliar voice before I saw his face. "You are right, David. Someday I must tell you the legend of Raven and the halibut hook. It teaches us that deceit is a two-edged sword. It brings grief to the oppressor as well as to the oppressed." I turned to see the speaker wink at Magdalena. He turned to me. "You have no champagne, Wynne. Come, let's remedy that." As we turned to go, David, deprived of his spotlight, shrugged and turned back to his group.

"Very smooth. Have we met?"

"Afraid not. My name is Royal Tagiloff. Magdalena is my first cousin. We grew up together in Ka'saan, a little village west of here."

"She's talked about Ka'saan in group."

"Ah, yes. The women's group you lead. Magdalena has blossomed since joining."

"She does seem to be dependent on David."

"Deplorable choice. But she seems happy. I've spent a few painful evenings with him. Painful for me, that is. I wanted to get to know the man my cousin loves. I like his work, but his ignorance is appalling."

We sipped our champagne and watched Magdalena and David, arms entwined, sipping Cokes.

"You look like Magdalena, Royal."

"You think so? Aside from the racial characteristics of black hair and dark eyes, I don't know that we share much else."

"You're both tall and slender."

"The Russian blood, I suppose. Tlingits are generally built closer to the ground. My great-grandfather was quite short, with very powerful shoulders. He could outpaddle anyone in a canoe."

I was disappointed when Tyler appeared. "May I have a word with you, Wynne?" At least his eyes broadcasted an apology to us.

Royal raised his glass. "Until later, Wynne."

I nodded to Royal and, walking away, growled at Tyler. "Not the best timing, Tyler."

"I'm sorry, Wynne. I'll make it up to you somehow. Let's talk in my ofice."

No bigger than a closet, Tyler's office held a tiny desk, two rickety chairs, and a battered filing cabinet. Glossy color posters announcing shows papered the walls.

Leaning forward on his chair, Tyler exhaled heavily. "I feel like my life's work is going down the drain. David is not cooperating."

"With you?"

"Yes, with me. He is being obstinate and I think it is because of her."

"Magdalena?"

He pulled a joint out of the desk drawer and lit it, blowing smoke toward the ceiling. "She's not as sweet as she looks."

"Tyler, I am in the dark. What is happening?"

"Oh, God, Wynne, will you listen to me? I don't know what to do. For years I've been trying to make this gallery pay, trying to get some recognition for what I've done. . . ." He inhaled deeply and held the smoke in. "The International Exhibit in Paris likes David's totemic work. I've sent them slides of different artists' work for years and this is the first time they've expressed any interest."

"But doesn't that make you happy?"

"It did. Oh, yes, it did. It meant his work hanging in the show and my gallery recognized. International recognition. I'd kill for that, Wynne. After my failure in New York, I thought I'd never succeed. And now it's so close. But David is balking. That fool!"

"I agree with that opinion."

Tyler raised his eyebrows at me while inhaling mightily. "Yes, I know how you feel about him. But what matters is his work. And he's slowing up his production. Talks about doubting his 'right' to do Tlingit totemic work. And that's the work they want. The whole thrust of the Paris exhibit is the universality of ethnic art. They don't want his goddamn bears."

As much as anything, I was shocked by his profanity. I don't think I had ever heard him swear. "How much of his work do they want?"

"As much as possible. They want to pick and choose. Plus, they want a stone lithograph. He hasn't even started that yet. And the exhibit is less than six months away."

"There are all sorts of reasons for producing less, Tyler. I remember when Jake slowed down. He was more interested in the perfection of each piece than he was with his output."

Tyler glared at me. "I know why he's producing less. To improve his bargaining position. The less work, the more valuable each piece. I'm the one who should make those decisions."

"It sounds as though you don't know what to think, Tyler. Why don't you talk to Magdalena?"

"I did. God, she was so oblique. These Tlingits, Wynne, they never say anything directly. She said she was glad that I was handling the work because I would get it to a wide audience. She thought it more fitting that a Tlingit do totemic work, but she said David was very sensitive to the cultural implications. David sensitive! Ridiculous!"

For some reason I was finding it difficult to be empathic with Tyler. Maybe because it was after office hours, maybe because he had dragged me away from the most interesting man I'd met in years, maybe I couldn't bring myself to care. I felt guilty and resolved to try harder. "Hmmm."

"David has less sensitivity than skunk cabbage."

"You think he doesn't feel?"

"It's not that exactly. It is just that he is so tied up in himself that he doesn't understand the problems of other people."

"Such as yours."

Tyler searched my face for irony and didn't find it. "Such as mine."

A thought came unbidden to me. "Tyler, I wonder if David might be slowing down because he fears success."

"That's nonsense, Wynne. Why should he fear something he has spent years chasing?"

"It's a real phenomenon. For many people, the elusive quality of success is the carrot. The reality of success can mean change."

"Wynne, that sounds like so much drivel."

"Tyler, did you drag me in here for my expertise or because no one else would stand for your abuse?"

A stricken look appeared on Tyler's face. He grabbed both of my hands with his. "I am sorry, Wynne. I don't know what I'm saying. I am so upset. Here I am driving away the only person who can help me. Please forgive me."

I softened toward him then but felt I couldn't give him much help. "Tyler, if you have talked to David and talked to Magdalena, I am not sure what else you can do. It really isn't in your hands anymore."

He bent his head. "I know. I suspect that that is what is really bothering me. I have no control."

I left him there in his boxy office, head in hands. I made my way around the walls, liking much of what I saw. I stopped near one painting that intrigued me, waiting for the couple in front of it to move on. Instead, they slashed at each other in whispers loud enough for me to hear. Their clothes pegged them as "after-the-oil-gushed Alaskans," members of the Gucci-loafer and silk-dress crowd, painted nails and tanning-bed complexions. I eavesdropped shamelessly. The painting was powerful. In it a Haida woman leaned languorously against a log in a rain forest.

From her lower lip an ivory labret protruded, a large one. She held a brown leather briefcase in her neatly manicured hands. She wore a navy-blue suit with a softly bowed foulard tie. On her head rested an extraordinary headdress with four curved horns pointing upward. No smile creased her solemn face.

I heard the woman speak first. "His work makes their culture less primitive for me."

The man hissed at her. "What a xenophobic thing to say."

"I can't help what I feel. They don't seem really civilized to me, even now."

"I can't believe you're saying these things. Were the Nazis a civilized race?"

The woman firmed her pink chin and faced him. "You're always trying to trap me. The Tlingits did have slaves in the eighteen eighties."

"So did we. Remember the Civil War?"

"That was different. And anyway, they didn't even have a written language until recently."

The man shrugged his padded shoulders. "Different cultures develop differently."

"You're always so goddamn tolerant. I hate it."

"And I hate it when a whole culture is not valid unless a white artist interprets it for you."

They moved away then, perhaps aware of my proximity. If art is meant to involve, David's show was succeeding.

All of the totemic work displayed red stickers. If David sold everything, what would he have left for the Paris exhibit? I shook that thought out of my head. I did not plan to make it my problem. Looking around the now thinning crowd, I waved to Sonja and Michael, who were whispering excitedly in a corner. He grinned impishly at her, which probably meant he was baiting her. Although he admired her work as a painter wholeheartedly, Michael never missed a chance to antagonize her. Pigtail in the inkwell, I think. She shook a paint-specked finger at him and stalked away. He pulled out a notebook and scribbled in it. As the only art critic in Juneau, he attended every opening. He waggled his fingers at me. I thought briefly about joining him but then felt Royal's presence behind me before I heard his voice. "Some of his work is glorious. I wish my enthusiasm for him were not so muted."

"He and Magdalena seem very close." I looked back at them, still leaning against each other.

"Or dependent. He has helped her a great deal."

"To do what?"

Royal handed me a glass and took a sip out of his before replying. "Magdalena likes you very much and I don't think she will mind your knowing about her serious drinking problem."

"That surprises me. She looks so serene." Somehow, I associate alcohol with erratic moods. Living with Jake had been like riding a roller coaster. Up and down. And wherever he went, he took me with him. I never knew what to expect when I walked through the door. "Magdalena always looks so calm in group and speaks so evenly."

"What looks to you as serene, Wynne, is quietly controlled terror. She is a shy woman who has difficulty in social situations. When she was a teenager, she found that alcohol helped. And then, of course, what followed is that her consumption prevented any kind of growth and therefore made the shyness worse." He turned to look at his cousin. His black hair, neatly plaited in a single braid down his back, did not look incongruous with the Irish tweed jacket. At least sartorially he blended the two cultures. The sterling cuff links in his pale pink button-down-collar shirt were, like David's earring, totemic. But Royal's represented the other moiety, the Raven clan.

He turned back to me. "We went to Edgecombe together. There we met Native kids from all over Alaska." He shook his head, remembering. "We were all so homesick, ninth graders away from our villages for the first time. We were all so full of hopes and ambitions too. Our parents thought, and we did, too, that attending high school led to entrée into the white world. We soon found out it was only the beginning of the struggle for acceptance and access to all of the things that non-Natives take for granted."

"It sounds as if Edgecombe was a school of hard knocks."

"On the contrary, we were protected in Sitka. It was only later we discovered the truth. That we had to become white to be accepted. Of course, that is only part of the truth." He smiled at me. "I am getting off on a tangent. I wanted to explain how Magdalena started drinking. It was at Edgecombe. There, it was a daring feat to even obtain alcohol, much less drink it. We were very well supervised. But she became part of a crowd that always took risks. A girl doesn't have as many options for expression as a boy does. I was involved in sports and Native politics. Magdalena spent time with her friends, who seemed always to be finding illegal ways to enjoy themselves. We drifted apart. She seemed more interested in beer than in family relationships. She kept up her grades though. Quite a feat. She was even accepted at the University of Washington in Seattle."

"She is very bright."

"That she is. But the university offered no haven for her. At Edgecombe she had security and acceptance. In Seattle she was just another student, and an Indian one at that."

"That made a difference?"

"It always does. Either people take you up because of exotic appeal or they dismiss you as an uneducated savage."

"Sounds rough."

"It is. And she had no defenses. Despite strong pressure, her parents neglected the Tlingit part of her upbringing. They didn't want her to be held down by the old ways. So without an anchor she really started drinking."

"She hit bottom."

Royal nodded. "I was at Stanford then. My aunt and uncle asked me to find her. She had disappeared. I searched for her for a week. Finally found her in a filthy house in the university district, living with a disreputable group of losers."

I shuddered, imagining what her life must have been like. Royal noticed my reaction.

"I was horrified too, Wynne. I dragged her out of there, not without a struggle, and took her to a rehabilitation center. Miraculously, it worked. She actually stayed there for a year and then another year at a halfway house. She's a faithful AA member. Since then she's stayed dry."

I took another sip of champagne. It seemed incongruous

to be enjoying the very substance that has ravaged so many
lives. Royal took my glass back to the table to refill it. I
looked at David and Magdalena, still holding their Cokes.
They probably had to bring them. Tyler, like most Alaskans, denied the existence of the high rate of alcoholism by
providing only alcoholic beverages. When Jake was on the
wagon, he'd bring his six-pack of Coke to every function
we attended. When he fell off, it didn't matter. The
champagne bubbled thoughts of Jake to the surface of my
mind. When he had drowned three years ago, the edges of
my mourning were tinged with relief. I swallowed the
thought guiltily while I watched Royal step gracefully
through the crowd back to me.

He handed me a crab puff with my champagne. David's
success meant that Tyler could afford a caterer. Royal gestured toward David with his crab puff. "He supports her
efforts to stay dry. He doesn't drink."

"I noticed that. It's a side of him I hadn't suspected."

"Neither did I. When I asked Magdalena about it, she
did say that his mother is a recovered alcoholic. That
makes him aware."

"Everybody in Alaska ought to be."

Royal wiped his long fingers on a napkin. "Sometimes I
think Prohibition wasn't all that bad. My grandfather believes that both times it allowed Native cultures to flour-
ish."

People were moving toward the table and we moved
with the tide, ending up by the window overlooking the
Gastineau Channel. Our shoulders touched as we raised
our eyes to the white peak of Mount Jumbo on Douglas
Island. "Both times?"

He smiled, a slow, gentle smile. "When Alaska was

purchased by the United States, liquor was prohibited until the early part of the century. The specter of Custer and the possibility of an Indian uprising still haunted the national consciousness. Even though the reasoning was wrong, the result benefited the Tlingits. Alcohol affects a community in the same way it affects an individual. It stops growth."

"It seems to hit the Natives harder than the whites."

"Yes, it does. The longer a people are exposed to alcohol, the less pernicious its influence. The Greeks and the Italians boast fewer alcoholics than the Irish. Our exposure, compared to the Greeks' thousands of years, is minimal. Maybe one hundred fifty years."

I decided to plunge in. Three glasses of champagne had nudged me into a confessional mood. "My husband was an alcoholic. We were just beginning to realize it. I think he drowned because he was drunk, celebrating the catch. . . ." I should have realized I couldn't talk about Jake without crying. Royal's face mirrored my pain. He led me outside, there putting on my jacket and my hat as if I were three feet tall.

"Maybe someday you'll be able to tell me all about it."

He took my hand, again as if I were a child, and we walked in silence. Thoughts of Jake mixed in with the sweet intoxicating smell of the cottonwoods. The odor of the sea seeped in, stronger because the low tide exposed the golden-brown seaweed and purple mussels that clung to the rocks at the bottom. I remember the shameful feeling of relief I had when I first heard that Jake was dead. Before the terrible grief began. More and more, his work, which was never good enough for him, triggered a depres-

sion that he doctored with alcohol. One drink led to five-
and six-day binges. When he ran out of steam, he became
so ill that it seemed to him that his depression had lifted.
When he drank, he cared about nothing and no one. I
shivered a little, remembering.

We reached the hillside in a few minutes. Up two
flights of wooden stairs perched my little house. The sun
still filtered through the gray haze even though it was close
to nine. Few lights shone in the downtown streets right
below. The three- and four-story wooden buildings that
housed general stores and cathouses and emporiums follow
the shoreline around the base of the mountain and now
house T-shirt shops and souvenir places and cafés. Houses
like mine dot the hillside. Originally built for mining
families in the early 1900s, they now provide years of re-
modeling for their current owners. The only thing that
worked when Jake and I bought it was the plumbing.
When he drowned I renovated it for therapy. I think I was
a little crazy then, working feverishly, almost believing
that he'd walk through the door at any moment. After I
finished the interior I painted the shingles white and the
gingerbread trim sky-blue and rose, and the picket fence
white.

Royal and I slipped our shoes off in the tiny entryway.
Juneauites don't wear shoes indoors. Rather than a cultural
legacy, I think the wetness of the climate demands it.
"Welcome to my aerie." He stood very still, like an animal in the forest, moving only his head, scanning my
walls, every inch of which are covered with paintings,
right down to the floor. I like to think my walls are alive
with Jake's paintings and those of our friends and some

from my clients. "This tells me a great deal about you, Wynne."

"That I'm a soft touch? That's what my colleagues call me for accepting paintings instead of cash. I tell them the cash economy is dead. They tell me you can't eat paintings. They feed the soul, I tell them."

Royal nodded with understanding, still staring as he pivoted around.

I pointed to the table, where an old photograph of my grandmother sat. "My grandmother would have taken the paintings, I think. She became weary with the killing and plucking of the chickens my grandfather accepted instead of fees."

"Was he a psychologist too?"

"No, a lawyer with a predilection for the little people, the ones with no money and many grievances and skinny chickens. I seem to have inherited his caseload fifty years later."

Royal followed me into the kitchen. A small dark hellhole for some miner's wife toiling in her own mine, I had opened it up by replacing the back wall with enormous French doors set with thermopane glass. We looked out at the hillside into a wild tangle of alder, devil's club, fiddlehead fern, dogwood, mosses, and wildflowers—sweet rocket, columbine, forget-me-nots, and shooting stars. I reveled in the light that reflected on the stuccoed walls and Italian tiles as that poor miner's wife could never have. Once the kettle had boiled we moved back into the living room with the tray. We sipped our chamomile tea facing each other on matching slipper chairs that were thickly padded and covered with orange tiger lilies. The low table between us I had painted in blue and cream. On it sat a lit blue taper and the tray with the teapot and the honey.

He crossed his legs, still studying my collection.

I tucked my feet in. "Ka'saan must be an idyllic place for a child."

"It was a happy place for a child, I think," he said. "No more than a hundred people, all related. Forest all around. Bays and streams for fishing. It was a rhythmic life. We moved to fish camp in the summer to catch and dry salmon. Then we picked berries in the late summer and fall. We relaxed in the winters. No dominant white culture except that we had a tiny school and a white schoolteacher. Yes, it was idyllic."

"When Magdalena talks about Ka'saan she sounds happy."

"Magdalena is just discovering her place in the clan, oddly enough. Her parents identified more with western culture than they did with their own. An odd thing, really. Her mother and my mother are sisters. Same clan. Raven. They went in different directions. My grand-mother, also a Raven, was obsessed about the loss of our culture. She encouraged everyone in the village to do something to keep it alive. It was our isolation and her work which made Ka'saan into a seminal place for Tlingit culture. We have skilled storytellers, dancers, basket weavers, bead workers, and carvers."

"I was surprised to hear that the ferry doesn't even dock there."

"How did you know?" he asked.

"Magdalena mentioned it in group. Says it's the reason David can't visit there. He refuses to fly in small planes and they know no one with a boat to take them there."

"How can a wildlife artist get into the wilderness if he won't fly in small planes?"

"I think he paints from photographs."

"No wonder his animals look so lifeless."

I poured more tea for both of us. "Is that the Tlingit talking or the art historian?"

"Perhaps the Tlingit. We have a special relationship with animals which is expressed through our clan groupings, our legends, our spiritual philosophy. We have depended on them for many things, food and clothing . . ."

"And earrings! I coveted the pair Magdalena wore tonight."

"Bessie made them. She is a very old lady in Ka'saan and a very skilled beadworker. The next time I go there I'll bring you back a pair."

If hearts can sing, mine did. "I noticed David wore an earring tonight."

Royal's face darkened. "I dislike that, that claiming of another's culture. It was an Eagle, which is appropriate since Magdalena is a Raven. But David is not a Tlingit and has not been adopted and is not entitled to clan insignia. I suppose I shouldn't let his pretensions bother me, but they do."

I was surprised at his vehemence. He seemed so controlled otherwise. I passed him the honey. No sounds disturbed our pool of quiet. He looked like a giant bird of prey crouching tensely.

"Why is an Eagle appropriate for David? The system seems complex to me."

"I think you have to be Tlingit, in the same way you

have to be southern, to know what a third cousin twice removed is." He relaxed, no longer looking fierce and vengeful. "Anthropologists call our custom of marrying outside the clan exogenous. It is a prudent method for keeping people healthy by avoiding consanguineous marriage. Two basic complementary tribal subdivisions exist: those who are Eagles and those who are Ravens. Being matrilineal, we take the clan of our mothers. Magdalena and I are both Ravens since our mothers, as sisters, are Ravens. Our fathers are Eagles. If we intend to follow clan injunctions, we must marry Eagles. This rather simple division is responsible for an extremely complex network of relationships, all of which are maintained only when everyone toes the line."

"What happens when people marry whom they want to?"

"I am afraid the whole social system collapses like a balloon."

"It sounds serious," I said.

"It is. Some people say it is necessary so that the Tlingit people can become Americans in the same way the immigrants did. Others feel the loss of an entire culture keenly. My grandmother, of course, thought it dishonorable and shameful."

I held back from asking him how he felt about it. I didn't want to be disappointed, not yet. We brushed cheeks good-bye and I hummed as I went up to bed. He did look promising.

CHAPTER 2

A week later, when I pulled up the blackout shade by my bed, the sun filled the tiny attic room. I dressed quickly in one of the few summer outfits in my closet, a creamy linen pullover blouse and skirt that I had picked up Outside during my last trip. The average summer temperature in southeast Alaska is fifty degrees. I wear shorts as soon as it hits sixty.

Even though I arrived early, my partner, Jane, was striding around our office, smoking furiously. She was steaming, which wasn't unusual. Her wiry blond hair was already pulling out of the bun she imprisoned it in every morning. Tall and muscular, Jane embodies righteous anger to me. She specializes in battered women and sexually abused children. You wouldn't think she could keep busy in a small town, but she actually has a waiting list. She takes in the anger that her clients can't seem to feel at

what has happened to them. It fills her so completely that
I wonder silently if she identifies too closely to really help
her clients. I haven't worked up the courage to suggest
such a thing to her. I knew she had seen too much. That
morning she glared at me, clenching a cigarette between
her teeth. Her long legs carried her to the window. I
walked through into my office, knowing she would follow.

"The police were here this morning, Wynne. The place
was overrun with them."

To Jane, whose relationship with the police was barely
cordial, "overrun" might mean two. "One of your clients
finally file charges, Jane?"

"That will be the day." She snorted. "No, it wasn't
domestic violence this time. It was about someone in your
group, Magdalena Peratravitch."

"Hard to imagine her being in any sort of trouble."

Jane squashed the cigarette butt into the ceramic ashtray
on my desk. "She killed herself, Wynne. I am sorry."

I reacted as people always do with death. Disbelief. "She
couldn't have. I just saw her at the opening a week ago.
And our group is today."

She had calmed down, now that she had told me, and
dropped into the padded rocker. I sat down slowly on the
pink love seat. She rocked, I pondered.

"I am at a loss, Jane. Somehow, I can't see her as suicidal. I suppose she may have been depressed . . ."

Jane, now that we were down to cases, put on the
glasses she kept hanging on a gold cord around her neck.
"It is very difficult to diagnose depression in a group situation unless the symptoms are severe. How many times
have you seen her?"

I thought back to our weekly sessions. "Three times,

maybe four. She was Tlingit and not naturally gregarious, so she didn't speak much. But . . ." Something tugged at the corner of my mind. The Coke. That was it. And what Royal told me. "She was an alcoholic. But on the wagon at the moment."

"Aaaahhh," Jane exhaled slowly, leaning back against the roses blooming on the upholstery of the Lincoln rocker. She rocked gently. Our minds worked together in a vermiculated pattern. Alcoholism changes everything. Conventional wisdom dictates that people don't kill themselves out of the blue . . . unless they are alcoholics. Logic becomes meaningless then. Alcoholism creates confusion and doubt and depression. I had watched Jake go through it.

"I worried about Jake sometimes."

Jane nodded. "I know. So did I."

I wrenched my thoughts away from him. "Had Magdalena been drinking?"

"So the police said. She dove off the ferry dock at low tide."

"What a risky way to go. She might have crippled herself for life."

Jane leaned back, khaki-clad legs crossed, a scuffed penny loafer dangling from one bare foot. "I had a client who swallowed lye. Had horrible internal problems until she finally did it right. She used a gun the next time." She closed her eyes. "And then one who took pills and went into a coma. She lived in a nursing home for another three years. And then one who hung himself. That was final. I even found a client once who shot himself. What a bloody mess. Brains all over the rug."

I wasn't surprised by Jane's memories. She either knew everybody in town or knew something about them. She left only once to go to Harvard, the mecca for Alaskans. I wasn't even surprised by the next thing she said. "David must be devastated."

"You know him?"

She opened her eyes. "Not in a professional capacity. But we have talked. Yes, we have talked."

"Well, what about, for God's sake? If it wasn't confidential, spill it."

"I'll get some coffee first. I made it when I first came in."

Once we were settled with our mugs of Costa Rican coffee—Jane would not allow Colombian, the sweat and blood of oppressed peasants—she told me about David. "I believe I first met him through a client who was living with him. She had been in a dreadful situation with a violent husband and moved in with David as a way out. He took her in out of compassion, I think. No love there. When she returned to her husband, David was concerned and made an appointment to talk to me about it. He hoped that I would be able to convince the woman— Cheryl was her name, they all have such little-girl names—to leave her husband. I remember that David did not particularly want her back with him, just away from the jerk who beat the stuffing out of her regularly." Jane lit a cigarette and puffed rapidly, gradually slowing down. She rocked gently, holding her knees. "He talked about his own family. His father beat his mother frequently. He witnessed it from the time he was very young. Surprisingly, she never hit David and wouldn't allow her husband to touch him. They were very close. His women friends all seem to be wounded birds that he helps to heal."

"That doesn't sound like the David that I know. He's a pompous ass."

"Oh, I know that, Wynne. That's a mask. He does feel deeply."

I couldn't believe it. I curled up on the couch, burrowing into the gingham pillows, and sipped my fragrant coffee. Even though I didn't agree with Jane's opinion of David, I was swayed. For all that she overidentified with her clients, she was a very skillful observer. People are transparent to her.

"But Magdalena's alcoholism, Jane, how does that fit?"

"What is this, Wynne, Psych 101? You know that substance abuse is just a continuation of abuse from the hands of other people. I don't know Magdalena's history, but I'll bet we'd find sexual or physical abuse in her childhood. As for David, my impression is that he is a binge drinker and generally stays on the wagon."

"Was there alcoholism in his family?"

Jane flipped her hand back hard, a sharp gesture which, with her, meant "of course, you idiot." "There always is. His father drank on payday and through the weekend—that's when he beat her—and his mother sipped wine from morning till night. According to David, she was always half in the bag. Numbed the pain, I guess."

We sat together in silence for a few minutes, the only sound the soft ticking of my brass ship's clock on the wall right above the matching barometer. Jake had given them to me after a good season. He said they would remind me of him when he was out fishing. And they did.

Jane broke my reverie. She pushed up from the chair and marched into our reception room. I heard her talking to someone. She refused to have a receptionist, saying that it would create a barrier for clients. She wanted everyone to have complete access to mental health care. I disagreed with her about the receptionist, but acquiesced as I did on other things like the coffee. The price of working with Jane was high, but generally worth it for her insights. I felt drained already, as if I had just completed a grueling session. And it was only nine o'clock. Jane poked her head in. "The police will be by later and your first client is here."

I jumped up to greet Phillip, a man in his fifties who couldn't hold a job for more than a few weeks. In a town where good jobs are plentiful, his disability stood out. He wanted women to stay home to lessen the "unfair" competition. Still stuck in the blaming stage, he hadn't yet faced himself. It puzzled me how he lived, as he seemed to have enough money to get by in an expensive town. He greeted me with an expansive grin and shuffled into my office.

"I brought you a croissant, Wynne. I know how much you like them."

"It beats me how you can come up with the cash to pay for these lovely presents, Phillip."

He tapped his head. "I have friends everywhere."

"And they all happen to be women."

He winked at me and we slipped into our roles, me questioning and reflecting, him pondering and struggling. When he left after an hour, I felt refreshed and ready to face anything.

✱   ✱   ✱

Young and full of puppy energy, the two police officers asked me all the standard questions. Was Magdalena depressed? Would I call her suicidal? Had she ever said anything to me about wanting to end her life? Neither man could sit still. They called me "ma'am" every time they addressed me, and they wiggled on their chairs, eager to get back to real crime. Their last question concerned Alex Day, the museum director. Magdalena had been at a party at his home right before she died. Although I emphasized my doubts about suicide, I realized at the same time how very little I knew about her. When they departed, talking about reporting back to Officer Manzoni, my office seemed to echo with emptiness.

That afternoon I left early to go to the indoor pool for a swim and a sauna before my group sesson at 5:00. I thought of it as my ritualistic purification, readying myself for the unpredictability of the group. For once, it didn't work. Even though I had emptied my mind while swimming laps, the topic of conversation in the sauna was Magdalena's death. Five or six other swimmers lounged in their bathing suits on the hot cedar benches. I knew most of their faces—they were regulars—but none of them personally. A fat man with a shiny red face shook his head, and droplets of sweat flew off him in a dog's typical arc. As I climbed to my usual perch, the top bench, I heard two women talking. The younger one spoke first in reverent tones.

"Poor David. He's a changed man. He looks terrible.

Dark circles and shaky hands. I feel so sorry for him."

The older woman's voice was brisk. "But, of course. It is tragic to have someone you love die, particularly by her own hand. The guilt can be crushing."

A very young man shrugged. "The way I see it, man, is that people ought to be able to do what they want to do without worrying about other people."

The older woman retorted. "That is an irresponsible piece of nonsense."

She left. I wanted to, but didn't, hoping to hear some new information. I didn't, but a quiet man in the corner said something that made me think. He hugged his knees to his chest. "I wonder if she planned it. You know, she wouldn't have been able to do it if the tide were in. It's hard to picture someone reading the tide book to plan a suicide. The rocks would have to be uncovered. It kind of bothers me."

It kind of bothered me too. The feeling of unease stayed with me all the way through my shower and walk over to the Women's Resource Center. My group met in a small room there, furnished with old overstuffed chairs, all cast-offs lovingly covered in gay paisley and floral fabrics. Every print on the wall was the work of Georgia O'Keeffe, enormous floral tributes to women and their sexuality.

Each of us balanced a cup of coffee: Greta, her cool demeanor masking her immaturity; Helen, "into" astrology and appropriately dressed in a red gypsy skirt; Marie, graying, a displaced homemaker and a misplaced identity; and Lenore, pugnacious and confused about her sexual orientation. As I looked at them, I realized how unpredictable groups are. No one quite knows what will happen. A dyad is much more likely to conform to traditional expectations of therapy. A group can be a circus. This one was a bit odd. But then, they all are. None of them were ready for individual therapy, but they wanted to "test the waters." I think that all of them, with the exception of Greta, and including Magdalena, were just beginning to feel the limitations imposed on them as women. The first stage is always anger, and this group was no exception. They bristled with it. In psychobabble parlance, I acted as a facilitator. In my own mind, I refereed.

Softhearted Marie captured our feelings. "I know I should feel sad, but then, I didn't know her well enough to feel more than a pang. But that makes me feel worse— that I didn't get to know her. She must have been so lonely. Poor kid."

Helen tossed her long dark hair and flicked her red skirt. "I wish I knew what her sign was."

Greta broke in curtly. "Knowing her sign won't bring her back from the dead. She was down, she pulled the plug, end of story."

Marie was shocked. "Show some respect, Greta."

Greta had the grace to look a bit shamefaced. "Sorry. It's just that you didn't know her like I did. She was always depressed about one thing or another. It was a real drag for David."

The group looked to me for guidance. I fell back on empathy. "It sounds as though you know a great deal about her, Greta."

"David and I talk sometimes. Oh, he wasn't complaining, you know, but he did say that dealing with her problems kept him from working."

Marie leaned forward. "That sounds like garbage to me,

an excuse for not working. My ex-husband used to say he couldn't concentrate on work if he had to do stuff at home. What he meant was, I was supposed to shut up, cook his meals, clean his house, raise the kids, and never make any demands on him. Men are selfish."

Everyone in the group nodded except Greta. "David isn't. He was always trying to help Magdalena. He refused to drink because she was an alcoholic. I wouldn't be surprised to hear she was so drunk from the party that she fell off the dock."

Lenore, silent up until now, spoke with barely suppressed anger. "You can't have it both ways, Greta. Make up your mind. Did she kill herself or did she accidentally fall?"

While the group argued, I thought about what Greta had said about Magdalena needing David to help with her problems. It did sound plausible because of her alcoholism. I knew from my own experience and from AlAnon that alcoholics are egocentric, and need to control others because they are so out of control themselves. An alcoholic can be hell to live with. Before he died, Jake started doing things that enraged me. Checking up on me. Making it very clear that he wanted me home when he wanted me home, not when I wanted to be home. I remembered what my father had said in one of our weekly telephone conversations. "Get rid of him, Wynne. I know what the Church says about divorce, but it isn't worth it. Chuck him!"

I had been seriously considering it when he died. I realized that I was beginning to link Jake and Magdalena in my mind. I felt so guilty about Jake. I hadn't wished him dead, just gone. And he was gone too. Forever. At the end of the session Greta announced with just a hint of smugness that it was her last one. She felt great, she said, and able to continue on her own without group support. I suspected that she wouldn't be on her own for long. Magdalena's death had created a vacancy at David's side, a position she obviously wanted.

Diane, the director of the center, stopped me as I was leaving. Short and dynamic, she was addicted to high-heeled leather boots and was wearing an elegant pair with cossack-style pants tucked in. "Disturbing business, Wynne." She leaned back against the wall, arms folded, eyes half-closed, appraising my reaction. "Do you think she killed herself?"

"I don't know. I really don't know."

She tightened her lips. "Nobody I know thinks she did. People have been calling all day. Some think she was pushed."

"Why?"

"Who knows? In our society women are expendable."

I agreed, but couldn't accept expendability as a motive for murder.

Diane continued her thought. "Some man becomes angry with 'his woman,' he can't control his feelings, he sees Magdalena and substitutes her."

"I know you see incredibly ugly things in your job, Diane, but your theory sounds nuts to me."

She laughed, a real laugh, not forced. "I won't accept your diagnosis, Doctor. Male powder kegs litter the landscape in Alaska. They come with the territory. We have more wife beaters than any other state in the union. And I think we have more sickies. Don't forget the baker in Anchorage."

How could I? A respected businessman with a family,

he took his victims for a ride in his small plane, landed on a sandbar, stripped them, laced up his hunting boots, and then hunted them as if they were moose. Except moose are at home in the woods. None of his many victims had been. They ended up in shallow graves, their bones protruding out of sandy riverbanks.

"I really don't think a parallel exists, Diane. There was no attempt to hide her body."

She looked down at her polished toes. "Someone might have been clever enough to realize she would be taken as a suicide."

I called my father almost as soon as I walked through my door.

"Arthur, please move up here. I need you." It was a child's lament.

"You sound tired, Wynnie."

"I am. And sad. A client of mine killed herself, and somehow it is reminding me of Jake all over again."

"Aaah. I remember after your mother died, every death hit me hard. Still does, but it seems to get easier with time. No solace now, I know."

"No, it isn't."

"I'm in the middle of finals, Wynnie, but I could saddle my graduate students with that onerous task and come up."

"I don't want you to visit, Arthur. I want you to move up here."

I heard him sigh. "I want to be around you, too, but the university has me under contract for the next two years. Perhaps I could move up there for the summer and then we could talk about a more permanent plan."

Yes! That was exactly what I wanted. We talked for another half hour about his classes, my clients, Jane, his garden, and my garden. My heart felt weightless as I climbed the stairs to bed.

CHAPTER 3

G uilt surged through me the next morning when I raised my blackout shade. With solstice so near, the sun had been shining for several hours while I slept, and I'd missed it. Living in a coastal rain forest, where the precipitation regularly overshoots one hundred inches a year, creates sun neurotics. I carried my coffee outside to sip in between bouts of weed pulling. Even though the sun shone, the ground sent waves of cold through my jeans and long underwear. I wondered if glaciated soil always retained the memory of the deep cold that imprisoned it for thousands of years. The tiny purple crocus had already bloomed, the daffodils drooped on their way out, and the tulips proudly stood up straight. Looking at the glorious tints of salmon and cream and red and yellow, I remembered the day last fall I had spent kneeling in the mud in a driving rain planting bulbs. I sat on a sturdy tree stump on the other side of my wooden walkway, wishing the colors could make me forget about Magdalena and how she died.

A booming voice bid me good morning. Looking down the stairs, I could see only an arm waving. It was attached to a large woman in a black dress and black thick-soled walking shoes. Her black hair was pulled back in a cushiony bun. She walked toward me with firm purpose, in a slow processional step, a giant sharp-eyed Raven apparition. I stood up as she approached. She planted her feet far apart and stretched out her square hand. Her warm hand enveloped mine and firmly shook it.

"I'm Rita Manzoni, detective with the local police department." She surveyed my garden with satisfaction and then nodded as if confirming something in her own mind. "I know who you are and I've come to talk to you."

I was so surprised to see a female detective in a town where the only female officers are meter maids, I could only stammer. "On a Saturday?"

"Makes you think I'm dedicated, doesn't it? The truth is, both kids have Little League practice, which leaves me with an hour on my hands. You live near the park, and I thought, why not? Cops are always working, even when they're supposed to be off duty."

She accepted my offer of coffee. When I returned with the thermos on a tray, I found her pulling chickweed out of my border. She stared up at me with good humor. "Did you know you can eat this stuff? I've got tons of it to pull in my own garden."

I nodded. "Gardening is soothing to me."

She stared at me appraisingly. "I'll bet it is. Dealing with those disturbed souls all day would make me run for something calm and orderly."

I wiped some hair off my forehead with my glove and left a smear of black dirt that I could feel, gritty, above my eyebrows. "Don't you need something soothing, too, after a day of police work?"

"You need a scarf, Wynne. Like a peasant woman. Only way to keep your hair from tickling your face." She raised her coffee, looking down as she drank. "I do need something quiet and peaceful. I cook. I love being in the kitchen, drinking wine and turning out good food. My kids love me being there too. It makes them feel like they have a real mom. As long as I'm singing in the kitchen, they're happy. And it makes me feel normal."

"Doesn't police work make you feel normal?"

She laughed then, almost a belly laugh. "In a way, yes. I feel normal in comparison to all the bums I have to deal with. In another way, no. It sets me apart from everybody else."

It must, I thought. I certainly wasn't thinking of her as a person. Even though we were making all of this polite chitchat, I was still very aware of her profession.

"Does it make your children feel different too?"

She raised her head from my border then, one meaty hand tugging on a stubborn horsetail root. The movement was sharp. I had taken her by surprise. "Yes, it does. I should have known that you are an acute observer." She sat back on her heels, looking at the horsetail. It was the male plant, with pointy leaves bristling out all around. "They want me to be at home with them. And that is where I belong. But it just isn't possible. Their father is dead and we've got to eat."

"I am sorry."

"And I am sorry about your loss too. I know it is a cliché, but death is final."

We sat in silence in the warmth of the sun. A slight breeze lifted the swordlike leaves of the tulips. The same breeze brought the tangy odor of the sea, salt, and seaweed.

Rita was the first to stir. "Now to business. Magdalena Peratravitch was murdered."

"Murdered," I said as if it were a new word to me and I was trying to pronounce it carefully.

"Yes, she was killed. She struggled with someone before she died." Rita sipped her coffee and shaded her eyes as she scrutinized the hillside down to the little tangled streets of shops and bars that led to the dock where Magdalena had died. Every movement she made was large and expansive and at the same time curiously precise. "And I don't think it was some wino crazed with drink, which is the popular theory with the boys down at the station."

All at once I wanted to side with the boys, because otherwise the murderer might be someone I knew. "Why not a wino? Some of those men hallucinate every time they get close to a bottle. And generally their hallucinations are tinged with paranoia. Paranoids do kill to save themselves from perceived enemies." My theory sounded very neat to me. After all, the winos all hung out along the dock where Magdalena had died. They sat on the pier and watched the boat and floatplane traffic and furtively lifted brown paper bags to their lips. They looked harmless, but who knows?

Rita shook her head dismissively, her beautiful black glossy hair reflecting light when she moved. "The wino theory is the easy way out. They make good scapegoats. It could have been like you said, but we would have found the wino curled up in some corner talking about it. Dissembling is impossible for winos. Not enough brain left."

I looked at her more closely. She sat on the stump as if she were resting in her sunny garden a bit before heading back to the kitchen to stir the spaghetti sauce. But she sounded tough. I wanted to hear her talk some more. "Have you had experience in those kinds of killings?"

She lit a cigarette and blew the smoke up above her head. "Had a daily diet of it in Seattle. Worked for Homicide there for fifteen years. I have seen everything." She grinned at me. She was looking at her cigarette with disgust. "The kids won't let me smoke in the house. They think I'm quitting."

"*I* did quit. Sometimes I wish I were still smoking."

"I *am* going to quit." She said it as if she were talking to herself.

I poured her some more coffee from the thermos. "Isn't it sort of unusual for a police officer of your experience to be in Juneau?"

"Is that a polite way to say, 'what the hell are you doing here'?" She chuckled, a deep throaty growl, then became somber. "I applied for a job here for two reasons. I was getting dead inside, and I didn't want my kids to grow up in Seattle." She spread her hands and cocked her head to one side. "So here I am. I can leave my kids at the park by themselves, I sometimes forget to lock my door, and I am beginning to feel some life inside again. I am the only one

on the force who has investigated more than ten mur-
ders—and in this one I know it wasn't a wino."

"Could it have been someone temporarily violent who
had been triggered in some way, not a wino, but someone
with an unstable personality?"

"That is a possibility. In most cases we'd still find the
person quickly." She stared at me probingly. "Who do you
think killed her?"

I bent over the dirt and pulled weeds and broke up
clods. "I don't know. I can't quite get used to the fact of
her having been killed rather than killing herself or having
an accident." I felt churning inside of me, a kind of sickish
excitement. "And evil is hard to spot."

"You're the first psychologist I've met who believes in
evil."

"I was raised Catholic. I believe in good and evil. I have
even seen evil." A small shudder shook me. Once you have
seen the face of evil, you are changed. The world looks
different, not so pretty.

Rita nodded as if she read my thoughts and agreed with
my conclusions. Then she nodded again. "Wynne, I need
your insight, your expertise on this case. I need your
help."

"How can I help you?" I wailed. "I don't know anything about police work."

"This is a small town. You are a small-town psychologist. You knew the victim. You know the people around
her. You may even know the murderer."

This is what I really wanted all along. I hadn't admitted
it to myself, but when Rita said it, I knew; I knew that I
wanted to find out what had really happened. Psychol-

ogists are always thinking about causes and reasons and motives for behavior. It is an automatic tic. Here was a chance to get inside a situation and not just tease it out verbally. Yes, yes, yes! "I do want to help. Her death affected me on a deep level. I want to find out what happened to her." Then I told her about my conversations with Diane and Tyler.

As soon as she left, striding away as purposefully as she came, I telephoned Jane. "Somebody murdered Magdalena, Jane. She didn't kill herself. She didn't fall off the dock."

I heard her sigh, almost with relief. "Somehow I can accept that better. I don't know why. How do you feel?"

She always plays the psychologist, even with her partner. "Energized. I'm going to help. Officially, that is."

"Fraternizing with the enemy," she said dryly.

"Jane, this isn't the time to debate about the role of the police in a democratic society." I wanted to get back to my garden. "What shall I bring to the party tonight?"

"That really helps me, Wynne. Anything to munch." Her voice warmed up with my offer.

Balancing the tray with the whole baked salmon and knocking on Jane's bright red door defeated me. I finally kicked the door and it swung open. Jane lives a few blocks from me in a cooperative apartment in an enormous old house. She and five others converted it into six units and manage to get along surprisingly well. All being members of the "helping professions," they at least espouse the ethic

of cooperation. Jane took the pan from me with an ex-
clamation of delight. I followed her into the living room,
where about fifteen people crowded on red and white foam
furniture and fat pillows. Cigarette and marijuana smoke
mingled. If anything, the legality of marijuana reduced its
use. Nodding to everyone, I received smiles and waves in
return. A few beckoned me to sit with them. Five or six
conversations created a din counterpointed by the music of
a jazz pianist. Everyone there worked in some sort of coun-
seling capacity as psychologists or social workers or sub-
stance-abuse counselors. No lawyers. Too cold-bloodedly
analytical. No doctors. Too unenlightened. No legislative
workers. Too disturbed. No arts people. Too playful. No
teachers. Too unionized. No laborers. Too rowdy. I stood
for a while, enjoying the sensation of the first minutes of a
party, not knowing what it held in store. Probably nothing,
with such a homogeneous group. I gazed at the walls instead of at the people. Jane's decorating motto must be "less
is more." On her beautifully painted snow-white walls,
every four feet or so rests an exquisite Eskimo or Indian
doll, dressed traditionally in parkas or kuspuks or tiny
Chilkat blankets. Their heads of ivory or caribou skin or
wood tilt in amusement at our human activities. Some hold
berry-picking baskets or harpoons or drums. I felt a pang,
seeing them pinned to the wall. Jane glided back from the
kitchen, handing me a balloon-shaped glass of wine.

She whispered into my ear. "Can we tell people?"

I knew she meant about Magdalena. I nodded, eager to
hear the reactions.

Too subtle to make an announcement, Jane drew Diane
aside. Sensitive to changes in the atmosphere—after all,

feelings are our métier—everyone in the room watched as Diane's face hardened, not with disbelief, but with resolve.

Frank, who worked with abusive men, was the first to notice. "Diane, you look upset."

She nodded once, eyes bulging with anger. "Magdalena was pushed. I knew it. Every woman I talked to knew it. Now the police know it." She glared at Frank, who was a close friend of hers.

Frank looked down, his soft brown eyes shaded. He'd been in this situation before, taking the rap for every violent male in the universe. Guilt had propelled him into his profession. "What a terrible loss." He looked up at Diane. "I know she wasn't involved with anyone I work with."

"You can't know that, Frank." Diane challenged him.

He smiled slightly. "You know our program. Nothing escapes my attention and we have no secrets."

They stood just a few feet apart, Diane's body tensed as if for a fistfight. "You can't know everything. And anyway, she didn't have to be involved with anyone. She could have been a convenient . . . target."

Frank rubbed his temples with his long fingers. "I'd bet my life on it."

"Your life is never at risk, Frank. You're male." Diane's voice grew louder.

"It was once, Diane. In 'Nam."

After a long moment, during which we all held our collective breath, she put out her right hand. He shook it and they walked with arms around each other into the kitchen. No one spoke. Then I heard someone murmur "Hepburn and Tracy."

I stayed long enough to help demolish the salmon I

brought. After a winter of canned and frozen salmon, fresh fish revitalizes. No wonder the Indians threw back parts of the salmon they caught, and the Eskimos, too, held an annual Bladder Festival to ceremonially throw back into the water all of the seal bladders left from the seals they consumed. Gratitude. Fresh game tastes like pure energy and seems to work that way in the body as well.

Jane saw me to the door. "Don't start," I cautioned.

"Okay, okay, working with the police is a swell thing to do, even though you might start thinking like them."

"Jane," I warned. She made a prayerful obeisance and backed away. I blew her a kiss and glided through the late-night sun, full of salmon energy and wondering how I could possibly fall asleep when the whole universe shimmered with glorious light.

CHAPTER 4

I prowled restlessly around my house that night, finding it impossible to settle down. The night air beckoned me. Now near midnight, it felt cool, about forty-five degrees, and smelled so pure, with no overlay of auto exhaust. I pulled on a fisherman's sweater from Ireland and strolled down to the dock with my hands jammed deep into the pockets. My rubber moccasins made no sound on the rough boards of the pier where Magdalena had died. Even at midtide, eight or ten feet of green water lapped against the weathered pilings wrapped with seaweed. Though I couldn't see them through the water, I knew that sharp gray rocks crusted with barnacles covered the area below the pier. I tried to visualize her death and found it made me sick to imagine how it must have felt. I wondered if she was unconscious when she fell. I hoped so.

I sat down on the square-cut log that ran the length of the pier, about ten inches high. No other barrier prevented anyone from throwing someone over or someone falling over. No railing. Nothing. And probably no one around to prevent it from happening either. On one side of the pier stretched old warehouses, for the most part deserted. On the other side a park stood, heavily used during the day, but not at night except for winos, who found shelter from the rain there. I could hear snatches of music and laughter from the bars uptown when the wind blew the sound toward me; lapping water made the only other sound.

I noticed a yellow light shining out of the second floor of one of the old warehouses that lined the shore. I knew that Sonja Werner lived there. In exchange for an enormous space, the company expected her to keep an eye on the place. I heard that she painted far into the night, fueled with a frenetic energy, pushing herself to the limit. I decided to risk a rebuff and called her name through cupped hands. She appeared at the top of a steep outside staircase, motioning me up in silence.

"I know you are working, Sonja, but I must talk to you about Alex's party."

"Why?"

"It was where Magdalena was last seen."

"Oh." She moved out of the doorway and motioned me in. "You're in luck, Wynne. I'm not making any headway on this damn painting. Come in.

"Coffee?" she flung back as she led me to the only seating in the room, two wing chairs covered in a floral chintz. They faced the windowed wall. Nearby stood a Chippendale screen that separated her lace-topped canopy bed from the rest of the room. She made coffee in the island kitchen. The rest of the space was bare, achingly bare to me, probably gloriously bare to her. She would feel claustrophobic in my house.

She carried the thin china cups over on a silver tray, with a graceful ceramic coffeepot, setting it all gently on a mahogany Queen Anne table between us. An ornate creamer and sugar bowl drew my eye. "Your eighteenth-century furnishings aren't incongruous in this modern setting, Sonja."

She looked at me with one eyebrow arched. "Classic design fits anywhere, Wynne."

So there, you cretin. I took a deep breath. I suppose I had to be polite in order to get information, but it would be a struggle. While she poured the coffee, I looked at the canvas on the easel near the window.

What was on it was bizarre. A triangular figure struggled with flags in front of a row of what looked like bicuspid teeth.

She noticed the direction of my attention. "I know you won't ask me what it means, Wynne. You probably don't have a clue, but neither do you want to be bored with yet another psyche, particularly that of an artist." She watched me intently with hazel eyes, a little frown of concentration on her freckled face. Her spiky red hair stood up in peaks stiffened by flecks of paint. I shrugged and looked around. The lighting mimicked natural light, illuminating the entire space. On the three solid walls Sonja's paintings hung. She once told me, "No one else can paint worth a shit." The fourth wall consisted of hundreds of small panes of glass, framing the channel and the mountains beyond, and the moon gleaming above. She continued to look at me appraisingly. "How come they all flock to you anyway? Are you some great therapist?"

"I may not be some great therapist, but I appreciate art."

"Even bad art?"

"Yup."

She stared straight across the water at the dark mountains outlined against the pale sky. "Do you like my work?"

"Yes, I do. I stopped buying it when the price went through the roof. Now I pick up an occasional print. If you ever want therapy, we can work out a trade."

She laughed, a short bark. She reminded me of a feisty terrier. "If I went to you, my work would suffer. Feelings fuel my paintings."

"Feelings?"

"Just like the other night, the night of the party. I was so angry that I painted half the night. I was crazy with anger. And most of the work was good." Her face reddened slightly, and she made a convulsive movement with her hand.

I put down my coffee cup, looking up at her. "Will you tell me about the party? I want to know everything that happened before Magdalena died."

"Why?" Sonja didn't use two words when one would do.

It wasn't because Rita had asked me to help her, I knew that. A therapist is not always skilled at sorting out her own feelings. "I'm not sure. Somehow, she and Jake are hooked up in my mind." I took another sip of coffee, which brimmed with caffeine, promising me a sleepless night.

Sonja held her thin lips tight and went to the window, her slight back to me, shoulders held stiffly. "Jake could paint. I miss him."

So do I. So do I. Grieving takes forever. For all of us.

She turned around. "Do you think she knocked herself off?"

"I know she didn't. The police say she was murdered."

"She stood up for herself at that party. First time I saw her step out of David's shadow." She picked up some brushes and an oily rag. "Might as well clean these. I won't get any more work done tonight." The smell of turpentine grew stronger as she talked. "I nominate Alex Day as the murderer. He is the most odious man I know."

I agreed, but didn't say so. "Why not a woman?"

She looked at me skeptically. "C'mon, Wynne, women don't kill women. Women kill men and men kill women." She scrubbed vigorously with her rag. "It wasn't a typical Juneau party. We were all summoned by Alex for a purpose. He wanted us to grovel."

"Who is 'us'?"

"Every artist in town. He also invited the board of directors of the museum and all of the gallery owners. Quite an assembly. Even Alex's pretentiousness couldn't disguise the hostility."

"Why hostility? I thought this was a party."

"A party with a purpose, Wynne. An official party. He even decked out two women in black dresses with white aprons to serve. If he had dared, he would have specified black tie." She gestured viciously with a brush. "Somehow, the museum obtained an enormous amount of money to purchase local work for an Alaskan traveling collection. After the collection is displayed in every major museum in the country, it eventually ends up at the Smithsonian."

"He made the announcement at the party, then?"

Sonja shook her head vigorously. "Oh, no, we all knew about it. He just wanted to dangle bait and watch us fight over it. Alex likes abusing power."

I knew that. The museum director never missed a chance to make others squirm. He also fancied himself to be irresistible to women, his attentions having forced more than one woman off the staff of the museum. The feminist community had been poised for more than a year for an airtight case of sexual harassment to blow him out of the water. I wondered aloud if he had been up to his usual tricks with Magdalena.

Sonja thought for a moment before replying. "She looked exquisite that night. She wore a creamy leather dress and some stunning jewelry made out of old Russian trading beads. She was excited, too, more animated than I have ever seen her. She moved around like a Tlingit princess." Sonja poured me some more coffee. I said nothing, not wanting to break her concentration. She closed her eyes, remembering. "There was something going on between her and Alex. But he wasn't coming on to her. In fact, he was treading very carefully around her. I remember thinking at the time that it was odd." She returned to cleaning her brushes. Although a keen observer, the mysteries of human behavior held little interest for her.

Her movements became jerkier. "All of the men were

currying favor with Alex and the board. It was sickening. When the board left, so did their good behavior. They started attacking me."

It was hard for me to imagine anyone attacking Sonja. I thought her inviolable as well as quite capable of taking care of herself. They couldn't have gotten away with much.

Sonja smiled, a wicked smile. "I suppose I fanned the flame a bit. I had been telling some board members about the difference between image and idea in art and how white male images have dominated western art for centuries and that ideas rarely come to the fore, chiefly because men are incapable of having them."

"What are white male images?"

Her expression became almost pitying. Barbarian, she thought. No wonder she was attacked. "White males think entirely in terms of possessions. Possessing women and property and children and houses and land and animals and other people who are not white. They express this world view through their art. They are obsessed with their possessions. And they try to make their obsession legitimate by objectifying it. Possessions as objects to be painted. They don't have ideas, and if they do, they don't know how to translate them into art."

"I don't understand."

She was impatient with my slowness. "Think about the work you see here in Alaska. Wild animals. Instead of hunting them and mounting them as a trophy, the white male possesses them and mounts the image on the wall. Landscapes of the wilderness. Instead of buying it and covering it with asphalt for a shopping mall, the white male owns it by putting it on his wall. Native people in traditional dress. Instead of exploiting them as he did in the past, the white male puts these primitive people in their colorful clothes on his wall for his amusement and as a reminder that he owns them. How many nude women are painted? Millions. How many nude men? Hardly any at all. By painting something, you possess it forever. It is yours. Even by buying such a painting you possess it." She pointed to herself. "I paint ideas, not images. I am not obsessed with possessions, not people, not animals, not land, not things. I am an artist. They are cartoonists."

I found it an interesting theory but didn't want to comment for fear she would take offense and kick me out. "How did the male artists react?"

"With infantile rage. It was delightful. Until they began attacking me and other female artists. They started out by wondering why no women ever become major artists. I said you might as well wonder why no slave ever became president of the United States. Then one said that surely some women have a certain measure of freedom. I said that women have been too busy wiping some male painter's ass. Then Magdalena jumped in. She said, 'Haven't you heard of Mary Cassatt or Berthe Morisot or Suzanne Valedon?' That stopped them for a moment." Her lips curled with satisfaction. "Then that jerk, David, exercised what he thinks is his male perogative. To keep his little woman in line. 'I've heard of those women, Maggie. But their work is nothing special. They just happened to be painting at a time when few women were. Even now, women are novelties as artists.' Magdalena looked stunned, as if she couldn't believe what he said, and ran out of the house. He looked embarrassed and went back to the champagne bottle."

"Was he drinking, Sonja?"

"Lord, yes, Wynne. This is Juneau, remember?" She was right to look surprised.

"What about Magdalena?"

"Of course. We all were. And drunk too. Even though the champagne wasn't that good, we all guzzled it. It looked like the kind of party where the guests start throwing glasses into the fireplace."

"When did the party end, Sonja?"

"How should I know?" She was still angry. "I left right after that."

I could see she wanted me to leave, so I thanked her for her late-night hospitality and walked home in the cool air. I suppose if Jake had been alive, I would have been at that party with him. He would have been angling for position along with all the other artists. And boozing right along with them too. Why did he drink? And why did I, a trained psychologist, not have an answer? I've heard all of the spiels: family history, race, environmental pressures, learned response to stress, avoidance of pain, genetic predisposition; but I still didn't know why he was becoming a drunk. The whys, in the end, don't matter. Finding reasons for alcoholism may illuminate the problem but not solve it. Suddenly, I was angry, walking fast, breathing heavily, seething. The cool air cut through my sweater. Jake died and left me alone. The rage sweeping through me left as suddenly as it came. I felt cold and tremulous. The wooden stairs up to my little house were slippery with dew and the ferns and the Sitka roses just starting to encroach on the railing. I stopped and touched the plants, the same ones that come back year after year. Their soft dampness gave me comfort.

Lilacs scented the air as I walked to church the next day. I made myself a mental promise for the hundredth time to plant a lilac bush at each corner of my house. The purple ones, not the white ones. The white ones look dirty to me, or maybe drained of color. I knew that I would inevitably be daunted by the knowledge that they wouldn't bloom for seven years.

The smallest cathedral in the world, a Victorian clapboard structure, gleamed with fresh yellow paint. Nothing, not even churches, is built to last in Alaska. Even now the idea of building with stone or brick seems like overkill. Maybe the history of boom or bust affects everything we do. Juneau might be a ghost town someday, just like all the others throughout the state. Maybe the glaciers will melt with the greenhouse effect and submerge us. My late-night visit with Sonja had left a residue of gloomy thoughts.

Rita was sitting in one of the front pews at mass with her two children, both of them wearing Little League shirts but for different teams. I watched them through the service. Both dark-haired, they were sturdy, smaller versions of their mother. She must have pointed me out to them, because at different times they turned around with shy smiles. Envy churned through me as I saw how concerned she was with them, turning to one and then to the other, finding the place in the missal, admonishing them for kicking the seat, guiding them up to communion. They rotated around her like planets around the sun. Jake and I had wanted children. After he died I think I was relieved not to have any. Now I wanted someone to care for and work for.

The congregation filed out of mass, shaking hands with the parish priest, standing around on the steps and the sidewalk, making conversation about the weather. Rita strode up to me and introduced me to her children, who asked if I "psychoanalyzed" people. I was surprised that they knew the word. The girl, Maria, said her teacher had told them about it in school and said patients laid on a couch and talked about anything for an hour. The kids had all decided it sounded too weird. What if you said something you didn't want your parents to know? What if you said a bad word? What if you had to go to the bathroom? Why would you do it anyway? Ricky nodded at everything his big sister said. She obviously held quite a bit of sway with him. Then, while they talked with some friends, I told Rita about my chat with Sonja.

Rita listened impassively. She had only one question. "Did Sonja see anyone leave around the same time that Magdalena did?"

I was embarrassed not to have asked that question. All I could tell her was that Sonja had left soon after Magdalena herself.

"I realize that you're not a trained investigator, Wynne. One of the keys is to ask as many questions as you can think of, particularly about people's movements and times. It can be tedious."

I could see that. I found it much more interesting exploring someone's perceptions than finding out at what time they did something.

After Rita and her children left for their games, I was paralyzed for an agonizing moment, not knowing what to do next. Emptiness engulfed me. Routine reasserted itself, and the Sunday paper came to mind. Thank God for habit, I thought as I strolled downtown to the drugstore. The Seattle or Anchorage papers might have come in on the early flight. With any luck, *The New York Times* would be on the shelf.

Downtown Juneau at noon on Sunday is quiet unless a cruise ship is in. Then the tourists swarm all over, in and out of gifts shops and the Lady Lou Revue and tour buses. I kicked at the trash littering the streets, the residue of a rollicking Saturday night. Everyone is sleeping it off, except the church folks, who dress up in their Sears-catalogue clothes and go out to brunch with the family in one of the restaurants specializing in all you can eat for $8.95. I stood on the sidewalk on the corner in front of the drugstore, soaking in the sun, its warmth undercut by a cold breeze blowing from the north. But I was warm, smug with satisfaction at having chosen wool to wear to church—I looked down at my slate-blue boiled-wool jacket, a plaid viyella skirt, and white wool tights. Even my white beret was wool. When I first came to Alaska I refused to wear a hat and muss my hair. Even though I wore warm clothing, I was cold that first year. An old-timer pointed out the loss of body heat through the head and suggested, in the interest of an intelligent response to climate, that I either change my hairstyle or put up with mussed hair. *She* even wore a nightcap to bed to guard against hypothermia. Since then I've amassed a collection of hats and mourn the passing of millinery shops.

Jostled out of my thoughts by a woman carrying newspapers into the store, I bought the *Times* and started back up the street. As I was passing the run-down old building where David's studio occupies the second floor, I pushed the door open, more on a whim than with an actual purpose. I started up the linoleum-covered stairs and at the end of a dim hall I knocked on his door. "Entrez," he said. Affected fool.

He stood at his easel with his back to a large dusty window through which some light filtered. On it rested a canvas with a romanticized oil painting of sea lions in a rookery, all of them looking far less malevolent than they really do. He stood back, posing, head cocked to one side, as if he were truly capable of examining his own work critically. Although he wore standard Juneau garb, jeans and a chamois shirt, he hadn't been able to resist a pink bandanna casually knotted around his neck and the tiny gold nugget that glittered in one earlobe.

As I came in he looked mournfully at me, lids drooping over his large brown eyes. "Oh, Wynne, I've been thinking about coming to see *you*, to pour out my grief. Magdalena was the love of my life, my inspiration." He dropped his head toward his chest, and then raised it slowly. "I find it impossible, absolutely impossible to work."

And I found it impossible to be empathic with David. He grates on me even as I sympathize with him. "I am sorry about your loss, David, and that you can't work. I imagine Tyler is upset about that."

"Oh, Tyler! All *he* thinks about is his commission."

"I thought it was more than that. His reputation as a patron, if you will, of outstanding talent."

He brightened at the mention of outstanding talent and then looked sulky. "All he wants is the Tlingit work. I *won't* do it anymore. I can't. It reminds me too much of her." His voice broke into a sob, and he turned away abruptly, taking a deep breath.

I looked around his studio. On one wall he had taped sketches on huge sheets of paper of animals done in heavy black crayon. I liked them for their unpretentiousness, a quality missing from his oils. On another wall hung his Tlingit work, five oils. I noticed that in each one a raven appeared. I slid over to take a closer look while David fought for composure. In my favorite, a Tlingit man crouched in a dance position, wearing an ornately painted Raven headdress and brandishing a carved dance rattle. His Savile Row suit fit him perfectly. The incongruity delighted me. When David turned back to me I was still smiling.

Red blotches marred his face. "Who could have done it, Wynne? Who could have committed this heinous crime?" He mispronounced "heinous." "She had no enemies. . . ." His voice trailed off, then picked up again. "Except maybe . . ." His voice faded again.

I was impatient. "Who might have been an enemy?"

David didn't look at me. He was staring at his painting. "Alex Day is a very strange fellow."

"Was Alex making passes at her?" Maybe she had threatened to expose him for his persistent attention.

"Oh, no, Magdalena would *never* have allowed that. She was an Indian princess, you know. Royal blood. She did say some nefarious activity surrounded the Greenwald Collection."

Even I, casual visitor to the museum, knew what the Greenwald Collection was. The most precious collection the museum owned, parts of it are trotted out once a year with great fanfare. The collection stems from 1867, when, immediately on the heels of "Seward's Folly," the purchase of Alaska from Russia, a U.S. naval ship had steamed up and down the coast. The crew's task was to explore its country's newest possession. As sometimes occurred, a naturalist traveled with them, a Johann Greenwald. Instead of concentrating on flora, Greenwald became entranced with the Native cultures. His notes alone are priceless as a written record of ancient cultures, even though the Tlingits and Haidas had been subject to considerable exposure from the Russians already, and had changed as a result. He meticulously recorded every facet of daily life as well as special ceremonies. At the same time, he collected hundreds of artifacts. I've seen parts of the collection. The sheer quantity is breathtaking. Apparently, his wealthy family bankrolled him. Greenwald acquired the choice pieces before the onslaught in the 1880s. Then museums from all over the world sent agents swarming to the Pacific Northwest and literally cleaned out the cultural treasure houses of the aboriginal groups. Priceless, the objects are without standard value now, deeply imbedded with significance. To gain prestige and capital the museum sent out parts of the massive collection to other museums for display. My father, a professor of anthropology, has had access to it in the past at different times, using it to help formulate cultural theories. He complains that since Alex became director of the museum, it is almost not worth applying for access because of all of the hoops one must jump through. Trust Alex to enhance his own power by diminishing others.

Nefarious activity. David's pretentious and almost vaudevillian word echoed in my mind. "Did Magdalena tell you what she meant?"

"Not really." He fingered the knot on his bandanna. "She was a bit secretive." He looked at me anxiously. "I am not criticizing her, Wynne. It was just the way she was. She was able to work on it only twice, but both times she worked far into the night, studying it. She became convinced that something was very wrong there. Her belief was that pieces were missing. She had been saying lately that she planned to speak to Ben Sinclair about it." He choked back a sob. "Oh, God, I miss her. Do you think this business was connected with her death?"

Yes. No. I don't know. I wondered about Ben Sinclair. The chair of the board of directors had only one ruling passion, which I suppose is enough for anyone. It was on the museum that Sinclair focused all of the knowledge and canniness he acquired in his years as a private art dealer. Ben's monomania turned a provincial little museum with one large asset into a very sophisticated organization with collections other museums vied for. I had a nodding acquaintance with him and knew far more than I wanted to know. He could probably say the same about me. Passing on information about other people is the price of getting along in a small town.

I left David in a trance, his eyes red-rimmed, fingering his bandanna and staring at his painting. He barely acknowledged my leaving. My own spirits picked up as I thought about my dinner guest.

CHAPTER 5

T he wind blew as I walked home, lifting dust and tiny bits of litter up from the street and sidewalk. I felt chilled, but for once I wasn't thinking about Magdalena. Instead, I planned dinner. Michael O'Donnell had been a close friend of Jake's and now was a mainstay in my life since his death. He had said he would bring halibut, but he might not remember. Brilliant and erratic, Michael was almost a cliché. When I stopped at the liquor store to buy two bottles of wine, no feelings of dismay assailed me. When Jake was alive we were still playing the game that everything was normal and normal people had wine with dinner. Since his death, buying wine no longer felt like a burden.

*   *   *

Michael popped through my door wearing a canary-yellow baseball cap and matching socks. "How do you like them, Wynne?" He pulled up a pant leg to display one more prominently. "Everyone at work hated them. They don't project the right image, you know. Buttoned down and serious—formerly Ivy League, now think-tank types." He twisted his visor around to the back of his neck. "They were much too polite to say anything. I am afraid they will drive me to greater depths, perhaps a polyester jumpsuit."

I handed him a glass of white wine in a goblet and took the green garbage bag from him. It felt very heavy. "I'll bet you didn't even fillet it."

He looked down at his sock. "I wanted to, I was going to, I really was. But they called me in today—typical—last weekend everyone scattered—some even to Hawaii—this weekend everyone works—no moderation."

"Then you fit in perfectly."

I dumped the contents of the bag on the kitchen table after I put newspapers down. Two black eyes stared up at me from a mass of gray skin. The halibut extended from one end of the rectangular table to the other. It must have been eighty pounds at least.

Michael, seeing my accusing look, held out his hands in mock supplication. "It was the smallest one the guy had. I swear. The rest were much bigger. I swear." He picked up one of the knives and started sharpening it. "The guy just tied up at the dock and there we were, a crowd of maniacs screaming for halibut."

"It didn't occur to you to buy half a fish?"

He smiled ruefully. "Never thought of that."

The mottled gray skin felt cool and sandpapery. It smelled fresh; that is, it didn't smell at all. Ripping the tough skin off with pliers, I was rewarded with a snowy expanse of flesh. Michael and I worked together quickly and an hour later had piled up a mountain of Ziploc bags of halibut. Elbows propped on the tiled counter, we toasted our butchering prowess with a Vouvray.

"Now to business," Michael drawled. "I vote for beer-batter halibut."

I groaned. "You always want batter, no matter what type of fish we cook. Let's sauté it in butter with wine and mushrooms."

"Would you like it better if I described it as 'an ambrosial dish, the delicate lace of the batter gently clinging to the tender chunks of fresh halibut'?"

"Have you ever tried writing one of those windy restaurant menus?"

He shook his head. "I get enraged with misspellings and syntactical errors on menus—spoils the whole meal for me." He poured more wine into my glass. "Anyway, I wouldn't get a byline. I may not make much as a critic, but at least I rate a byline."

"Jake treasured your critical review on his work. And by that time your column was syndicated."

Michael hooked his legs around the legs of the wooden stool he sat on. "I'm breaking into magazines too. I just sent a piece off yesterday to *Alaska Magazine* on Sonja. She won't speak to me after she sees it."

"That surprises me. I thought you had nothing but admiration for her work."

"I'm a critic, not a reviewer. And anyway, I do manage to imply that she is head and shoulders above anybody else in the state. She's the best we have. The only one who comes near is David Whitmore. His totemic work is stunning."

I shifted on my stool. "I think so too. But he says he can't do it anymore. Reminds him too much of Magdalena."

Michael drained his glass, holding it so tight that his knuckles turned white. "When I heard it, I couldn't believe she'd killed herself. I still can't. She was too vital."

"She didn't. The police say she was murdered." I told him that I was "assisting the police with their inquiries."

"God." He slumped down on his stool. "Why would anyone kill such an innocent? Her death really got to me. It was like Jake all over again. I finally made my peace with *his* death by accepting it as part of a natural pattern with the storm and all. But this is different." Tears glistened in his eyes.

I squeezed his hand. "It sounds like you were very close to her."

He managed a smile. "I guess I was, a little bit. I thought you knew. We talked about Art with a capital *A*. Much of what she knew was on the feeling level and quite accurate in spite of that. I couldn't understand her staying with David. . . ."

"I just found out she was an alcoholic. Did you know that?"

A startled look spread across his face. He shook his head. "She seemed so fragile to me. Not quite of this world. But maybe being poised between two cultures would make anyone an alcoholic."

"I also found out that David supported her efforts to stay dry."

"Maybe he isn't as much of a jerk as he acts."

"Did she talk about her life with David?"

He shifted on his stool, twirling his glass. "Personal stuff? No. Just art. Our conversations reminded me of my college days. They were of the sort that seem so meaningful at the time, but despite their earnestness, fundamentally puerile." He leaned forward. "Once in a while she told me what was happening in her job. I remember once we got into truth and morality." He moved away from me and put his hand on the porcelain stove. "Let's get on with it, Wynne. I'm starved."

"Hang on. Will you tell me more about the truth and morality talk?"

He grinned then with all of his teeth and I knew a deal was coming. "I'll tell you if we do beer-batter halibut."

"Michael!"

"All right, all right, we'll do both. We have enough halibut to try fifty dishes."

While Michael mixed the batter for his halibut, I cut it into chunks for the deep fry and into slices for the sauté. My knife slid through the fish almost without resistance. When he popped the pieces into the sizzling oil, the smell filled the kitchen. My mouth watered. There is something very seductive about hot grease. Then Michael dipped into the oil with a Chinese strainer and set the halibut cubes gently on paper towels to drain.

I snagged one piece that was perfect. Fish tender and very moist, batter crisp and dry. "Well, don't keep me hanging," I whined.

He turned around, catching me in the act of snagging another chunk of halibut, and looked smug. "I had been talking about how important it was that the artist paint only the truth, to even paint ugly, but avoid being swayed by the whims of the market."

I rolled my eyes. "Easily said by someone who doesn't make a living painting."

"True. But remember the flavor of this. College dormitory. God, it's embarrassing to recall it."

"Go on. What did she say?"

"She somehow leapt from *painting* what is true to *saying* what is true, no matter who it hurts. She seemed to get specific at that point, but I was confused as she hinted about exposure and public reaction. When I pressed her, she clammed up. So I let up. Maybe she was carried away by my sophomoric rhetoric."

I stopped cutting mushrooms long enough to drain my glass. "I wish you had pressed her. Maybe it wouldn't have made a difference, but I think she was talking about the Greenwald Collection."

Michael raised his eyebrows in question.

"David told me that she told him that the collection doesn't seem to be intact, that some of the pieces are missing. She planned to go to Ben Sinclair about it."

Michael's hands shot into the air dramatically. "Not the *Greenwald*. I cut my teeth on that collection. It was when I did Northwest history at Yale. They let me put together an exhibit of fishing artifacts." He swung off the stool and pointed to the halibut. "It was the halibut hooks that got to me. The perfect blend of form and function. It was then I realized that art could be everywhere, even in a fishing hook." He moved his head from side to side a bit drunkenly. "I love that collection." His words were slurred.

I slid off my stool. "We'd better eat. We're drinking too much." I opened the French doors leading out to the hillside and shooed him out.

While he sank into the lawn chair I melted butter in a copper pan. The earthy odor of young plants outside mingled with the rich buttery smell. I added the mushrooms and a pinch of tarragon and then the thin slices of halibut. As they cooked gently I grabbed the white ironstone plates out of the oven, and arranged the sauté. The green salad was already on the table outside. We chewed slowly and in silence, savoring our creations, looking only at our plates and at the tangle of leaves and vines and flowers on my hillside. Buttercup and fern and Indian rhubarb and sweet rocket fought for space. I kept tubs of nasturtiums on the deck and left the hillside to the wild plants. When we finished eating, Michael carried our plates back to the kitchen and returned with a bottle of wine and clean glasses.

"Last one for me, old buddy."

"Me too. I have to be bright and chipper tomorrow. We have a subsistence hearing."

"The good fight . . ."

"Luckily, the official stand is my personal stand. The Natives have to have special access to their food sources, no matter what our needs are. It's much more basic to them. They won't be Native anymore if they can't eat whale and seal and salmon." He bent down to kiss my cheek. "Don't get up. I love you. Be careful playing Nancy Drew."

He stopped, turned back, poking his head around the corner of the French door. "Something is bothering me about Magdalena's death. I think, oh, I don't know what I think . . ." And then he disappeared. Like mercury, you touched him and he scattered.

The next day the sun shared the sky with nothing. No clouds edged into the brilliant blue dome. At the end of a summer of almost constant light I am ready for the restful darkness, but now at the beginning the light invigorated me. While I made coffee and oatmeal I opened every window in the house to let the cool air sweep through, bringing with it the sharp tang of the sea. Wrapping up in a down robe, I sat on a stump in front of the house to eat my breakfast. The mountains behind the town of Douglas across the channel stood out against the sky as if cut out; snow still dappled their tops. A floatplane took off from the dock, quietly humming at first and then building to a roar as it cleared the water. Two cruise ships, pure white leviathans, waited patiently at dockside as their mature passengers streamed up and down the gangplanks. In crayon-colored clothes they chattered brightly to one another as they swept up and down the streets, in and out of T-shirt and fudge and gift shops, clutching maps and shopping bags and each other.

*　　　*　　　*

It was barely nine o'clock when I reached the office and Jane's hairpins were already sliding out precipitously. She swung around as I entered our reception room and put her hands on her hips. "It is foolish of you to help the police. They will just find whoever is easiest to charge with the crime and your efforts may land you in trouble with the real murderer." She paced around the room. "I just don't like it at all."

"I know you view it as collaborating, Jane, but I think I can help without endangering myself."

"It is *not* your job, Wynne. Your job is in here, listening to people, helping them to grow."

I looked at her. "Something happened over the weekend, didn't it, Jane? I can see that you're angry, but not at me."

She looked down sheepishly. "I am angry with someone else. A fifty-year-old man who molested a seven-year-old girl. Probably his fiftieth victim. And her mother won't let her testify against him because he is their minister. I want to kill him." She clenched her fists. "But I still think it is dangerous for you to do what you are doing. I don't want anything to happen to my partner."

I hugged her. "I am touched by your concern, Jane. I feel as if I *can't* stop. I don't know why."

She stepped away from me. "*I* know why, Wynne. Somehow, you are confusing Jake and Magdalena. You think that if you solve this, find a reason for it, then you'll believe that there is a reason for all death, including

Jake's. If only you had looked harder. Well, let me tell you, it won't work. Death and pain and misery are not part of some grand pattern. They strike anytime, anywhere, and there is no reason. Accept it."

Tears burned behind my eyes. "I can't."

She laid her hand gently on my cheek. "You have to."

By lunchtime I had regained some equilibrium. Work always helps. Jane walked into my office and sank into the sofa. "I think I have just about had it, Wynne."

I sat down beside her. "You can't take anymore?"

She shook her head, her lion's mane of hair completely free of hairpins. "I've been on the phone all morning to the D.A.'s office, the child's mother, the teacher she first reported to . . . and I haven't gotten to first base. Without the child's testimony there is no case." She leaned back, closing her eyes, one hand over them. "I've seen too much. I thought I could do this for the rest of my life, but it only gets harder."

"Maybe you thought you could get used to the horrors that people have to endure."

"Never," she said fervently. "These guys can go through a hundred children in a life span if they can get away with it. Age does not slow them down."

"What will you do?"

The muscles in her jaw bulged. "I'll nail him. After that, I don't know." She bent forward, her head in her hands. "Wynne, your partner is getting as crazy as your clients."

I had no comforting words for her. "How about coming to lunch with me? There's nothing more soothing than food."

Jane hesitated, then stood up. "Yes, that would be best for me right now. I don't want to be alone."

She revived out in the sunshine. She had slipped a tailored lime sweater over her melon-colored silk blouse. The off-white of her linen trousers provided a sober note. Her mood soared as we walked arm in arm along the crowded sidewalk, nodding to acquaintances. It was the lunch hour, and state office workers were everywhere, their faces like flowers tilted toward the sun. We headed to Lucille's by mutual and silent consent.

Ah, Lucille's. Haven for those weary of dining in chic little places where the decor, be it wood and ferns or neon and Formica, makes more of an impression than the food. Lucille's is real. Scarred linoleum floor, horseshoe-shaped counter rimmed with metal, mushroom stools that swivel, red-padded booths, hand-lettered signs, thick white crockery, bottomless coffee cups, and Lucille herself: a large-bosomed figure encased in a white uniform, topped with a magnificent head of strawberry-pink hair in which a pencil always rests.

I ordered a large plate of potato salad from Lucille and she shook her head for the umpteenth time, refusing to give me the recipe, not even when I offered her my secret recipe for killer brownies. Jane ordered fish and chips. The smell of hot grease grew more intense as the lunch crowd ordered their daily French-fry fix. Lucille's meals are starch based. I felt glad that she was finally being vindicated by the medicos who are touting complex carbohydrates as wonder foods. Finally, potato salad without guilt. Without *much* guilt.

David and Greta sat near us. Even though he looked exhausted, he still summoned enough energy to talk. Greta drank it all in, opening her eyes wider at appropriate intervals.

After a few polite murmurings about the state of her being, I asked Greta the question. "Did you know the police believe Magdalena was murdered?"

She nodded. "But why would anyone murder her? She didn't have any money."

"Greed's not the only reason for murder. She might have known something about somebody."

Greta leaned forward. "If you want my opinion, I can tell you. I think that Indian guy did it." David looked surprised, then thoughtful. I guess she hadn't shared her insight with him.

Royal? "Why would he kill her, Greta? They were cousins, part of the same family."

She tapped her head as if there were something of value inside. "That's just it, you see. We don't know anything about what the Indians really think. They may look like us and act like us, but they don't think like us."

I hoped to God I didn't think like Greta. "Even if their customs are foreign to us, Greta, I doubt that murder is one of them."

"That's where you're wrong, Wynne. The Tlingits are bloodthirsty. They even used to kill slaves during potlatches just to prove they could afford it."

"Sounds like you've been boning up, Greta."

She patted her hair. "I tagged along once on the museum tour that the Tlingit guy does. He told us all sorts of gory stuff."

David was definitely looking more haggard, but I didn't want them to leave yet. "What do *you* think, David? About Royal murdering her, I mean."

"Let it alone, will you, Wynne? Can't you see I'm grieving?"

He was beginning to look tearful. Greta looked daggers at me and gathered up her purse and David, and swept out the door.

Struck out again. I turned to Jane, who was playing with her napkin.

"I know you don't want to hear this, Wynne, but I have to tell you."

I resigned myself. "Shoot."

"Next to the military and the police, there is no more violent group than the family."

"Well, I suppose I know that, but it doesn't fit. What reason would Royal have?"

"Anger in families burns brighter and hotter than in other groups. It builds faster too. Fewer inhibitions among intimates. Strong emotions flare. Love turns to hate. There doesn't have to be a specific reason."

"Maybe that happens with the people you see, Jane. But the men who are violent are character-disordered. You can tell that a mile away. And Royal is not. He is solid."

Jane looked hard at me with her tell-me-the-truth-or-I'll-squeeze-it-out-of-you look. "You really like this guy, don't you?"

I toyed with the idea of playing down what I felt for Royal, but knew that I couldn't fool her. "Yes, I think I really do like him."

She only said, "Be careful."

I trilled to Lucille when I paid the bill. "I'll trade you my chili recipe, the one that blows the top of your head off. Give me a break, Lucille."

She didn't even look up from wiping the counter. "Not a chance, honey. How else am I gonna keep you coming in here?"

Defeated again.

A few days later I contemplated the grayness of the rain that drizzled out of the sky down the windowpane in between recording the running notes of the day. Late afternoon, low energy, and rain. The green and black screen of my personal computer bore no scars from the stories of misery, and tragedy, and downright bad luck it had seen. My last client of the day turned out to be an accomplished liar whom I forced to come in by threatening her. Her child, a fifteen-year-old boy, was suffering from a lifetime of hearing lies, big ones and small ones, from his mother. He knew it wasn't right, but had no defense against it. His aunt had referred him to me. The boy was beginning to doubt his own sanity because of the way his mother changed her stories to suit whatever mood she was in. The mother projected warmth and charm until I confronted her; then she became venomous, treating me like a snoop and a busybody, two of the milder names she called me in our endless hour together. I resolved to recommend that the boy be placed with his aunt on the basis of moral neglect. I hoped I could make it stick. I was still wrung out, bent over my keyboard, when Tyler suddenly appeared. He towered over me, looking seedy, a rare state for him. Normally a fastidious dresser, particularly by Juneau standards, his collar was rumpled and his damp halibut jacket had a torn pocket.

"Wynne, I am so upset," he burst out.

I led him over to the pink love seat and then dropped into the Lincoln rocker.

"About what, Tyler?"

"I can't sleep at night. Magdalena's death stopped David from working. He just plays with his brushes. He is not doing *anything*."

"Tyler, what's the rush? The man has to mourn her."

"Why can't he mourn and work at the same time? The Paris exhibit is almost upon us and I have nothing to send them."

"What do they want?"

"Anything that pertains to the theme of the show, which is the transformation of traditional ethnic art. They want a stone lithograph too. He hasn't even started on that!" I was surprised at his vehemence. Tyler usually thought being emotional was vulgar. Now his face had actually gone from alabaster white to rosy pink. He ran his hands through his thinning blond hair and looked with distaste at one of the paintings on my wall. A plump white unicorn cavorting in an Alaskan spruce forest, it was sentimental but funny. Tyler rolled his eyes at me.

"Tyler, what do *you* get out of this?"

He leaned forward eagerly, his knees almost touching the coffee table. "What I've always wanted. International recognition." He even looked vulnerable, his thin aesthete's face shining.

Then he stood up, pacing quickly, discharging his nervous energy in jerky bursts of speech. "David says he can't bear to work. I told him I can't bear his *not* working. Wynne, what am I going to do?"

"I don't know, Tyler. It sounds as though you have no control over what happens."

"That's just it, Wynne. I feel helpless. And desperate." He slumped down deeper in the settee.

I allowed myself to wonder if he had killed Magdalena so that David could work. *Was* the Paris show so important to him? Too many variables. No guarantees that David would work more with Magdalena gone. What was I *doing?* Suspecting a friend of fifteen years? What was wrong with my thought processes?

I left shortly after Tyler did, slogging home in the rain, feeling sorry for myself. The Sitka roses brushed against me as I walked up the slippery stairs, adding their dampness to that from the rain. After I started a fire in the woodstove I changed into a long rose-colored chenille robe with deep pockets and curled up in a chair, drinking peppermint tea with honey. When the phone rang, the sound didn't register at first, so deep had I sunk in the blue sea of depression. My father's voice boomed through the wire.

"How about meeting me in Fairbanks next month, honey?"

"What's the occasion?"

"I'll be giving a paper on kinship systems of the Haida at an anthropology conference there."

We made the arrangements to meet, and then I remembered Greta's description of Tlingits as violent. I asked my father what he knew.

His voice came slowly, shot through with authority as if he were addressing his graduate students. "It *is* true that the Tlingits fought many battles—with other Native groups, and with the Russians. However, their primary activity was trading. They were superb, traveling up and down the coast, controlling trade routes, keeping goods flowing. I would not describe them as overly hostile any more than I would describe the citizens of the United States as overly hostile even though we have been involved in many battles and are perceived as aggressive and violent. Naturally, my dear, generalizations of any kind are inaccurate."

The sound of the rain pattering on the roof lulled me to sleep.

CHAPTER 6

Gauzy gray clouds swathed the mountains as I strolled to work the next morning. The sound of a cruise-ship horn drifted from the water, signaling its presence in the thick fog in the channel. I sat on the dock for a few minutes, enjoying the unusual silence that comes when the town is socked in. If it lifted a bit from the surface of the water, I would take a kayak out after work and paddle around.

I telephoned Ben Sinclair, the chair of the museum board, during the noon hour. Then I stayed in, eating plain yogurt and fruit, working on a court report due the next day. Jane popped in and out, noticeably less upset. She had discovered another young victim of the preacher, and the mother wanted to avenge her child. Jane was gleeful. And Ben agreed to drop by my office after work on his way to dinner. His lovely fruity voice purred over the telephone; I didn't tell him any specifics.

Even though the periwinkle blue tea dress I wore was hardly wrinkled, Ben's scrutiny provoked me. He was of medium height, with thick white hair, and his rimless glasses did not disguise his sharp eyes, which appraised everything in the room before he held out his soft hand.

"You look lovely, my dear."

"My mother always said that beauty is only skin deep."

"Your mother missed the point."

His response reminded me of his criteria for friends—their looks. Intelligence, loyalty, kindness, meant little to Ben, only physical attractiveness. "I don't think so. I know we don't share the same values, Ben, but we do share a feeling for the Greenwald. And I think Magdalena's death had something to do with it."

"That little Tlingit girl? Preposterous."

"David told me she wanted to talk to you about something connected with the museum. Did she?"

He ran his fingers down his silk lapels as if to make sure he was still there. "Not exactly," he equivocated.

I wouldn't let him off the hook. "Not exactly? Either she did or she didn't."

"Well, she came up to me at that dreadful party at Alex's. It was too noisy and too smoky and too full of badly dressed people."

"Was anyone nearby when she talked to you?"

On his face was a moue of distaste. "Impossible to tell you. There were so many people milling around."

"What did she say?"

"She told me that the Greenwald was being looted. 'Shocking,' I said. 'By whom?' Then she gestured toward all of the people. 'Someone here,' she said. Then Alex joined us."

"She said nothing else?"

"Only that she'd see me in the morning."

"And she was dead in the morning."

"Regrettable, Wynne, but no concern of mine."

"But the Greenwald is."

"Surely you don't believe her attention-seeking little story, do you?"

That stopped me cold. I had to take a deep breath before I spoke. "I *can't* believe that you didn't check out what she said, you of all people. The museum is your life. And the Greenwald is the museum."

"You exaggerate, Wynne." He pulled out a sterling cigarette case, opened it, and offered me one. When I refused, he raised an eyebrow in question, I nodded, and he lit his, blowing smoke out in a thin, steady stream. I noticed they were British cigarettes. "She and so many of the Indians around here believe that we are out to get them and their precious stuff. To my mind, they're all paranoid schizophrenic." He leaned back then with a satisfied sigh.

I recalled that Ben had done quite well for himself buying ancient artifacts from Natives who didn't know their real value and then selling them for astronomical prices to East Coast dealers. I refrained from mentioning it or the fact that he had grossly misused a psychiatric term. I was beginning to understand the superhuman forbearance police officers have to have. "Isn't it possible that someone is taking articles from the collection and selling them to the highest bidder?"

He waved a hand negligently. "Highly unlikely, Wynne. Any museum would demand to know the provenance of an object, and as far as private collectors, well, not many in the world have the wherewithal to consider such a purchase."

He was stonewalling me. Before I could try another tack, he pointed to an early painting of Sonja's. "By the way, that is worth eight or ten thousand now, Wynne. Let me know if you ever want to let it go."

Sly old devil. He must have known that I would be needing a new roof soon. I refused to let him sidetrack me.

"What if whoever is looting the collection makes sure that a buyer is available, a buyer who will ask no questions?"

He stroked his white mustache. "Wynne, it just couldn't happen. That's all."

His obstinancy was puzzling. Perhaps he was involved. "Why are you so sure, Ben? *You* have that priceless collection, probably with lousy security. An employee says it is being looted, and you stick your head in the sand."

Looking down at his neatly manicured nails, he pressed his lips together tightly. "I can't begin an investigation without some sort of evidence. The publicity for the museum would be horrendous."

"You care more about the museum's image than you do about the artifacts."

"That's not true, Wynne. Too many people could be hurt."

"Like Magdalena. She certainly got hurt after saying publicly that someone at that party was a thief."

Ben opened his eyes wide and dropped his jaw a bit. "I just can't believe that her death is connected to the museum." Finally, something had gotten to him.

I rose from my swivel chair and walked to the window, where my view encompassed another old office building and the mountains and a bit of sky. "But you can't be sure about that, can you? You can't ignore her charge. What if someone finds out somewhere down the line that systematic looting has been taking place for years and you didn't do anything about it? How do you really feel about your precious collection being dismantled piece by piece?"

He held out his hand like an urban traffic cop. "Stop, Wynne. You have overwhelmed me." Looking at his very thin gold watch, he continued. "I must go, my dear. I promise you that I will look into this matter. Thank you for bringing it to my attention." Once more he was chair of the board, being gracious to an underling. He stood up and made fussy little movements down his clothing. "I'll call you when I know something, Wynne."

My shoulders felt stiff from the tension of badgering Ben into doing something. I slipped into the sweat suit I kept at the office and loped down the street to the rickety little building where the kayak rentals were housed. The fog had lifted up to the tops of the mountains, giving enough visibility to the floatplanes, but still acted like a lid on a stew pot. We simmered in the cool but humid air. The woman behind the counter didn't ask me if I knew how to use a kayak or even if I could swim. She handed me the life jacket and the paddle and pointed out a one-person kayak lying on the dock. We lowered it to the water with a hook-and-pulley system and I scrambled down a metal ladder, stepping gingerly into the fiberglass craft. What would the ancient Eskimos have thought? Being the practical people that they were, they probably would have embraced fiberglass in the same way contemporary Eskimos embrace Twinkies and satellite dishes. With aplomb. Survival demands flexibility. Once in, with my legs stretched out in front of me, I began paddling gently between the barnacle-encrusted pilings. I heard the woman shout, "Watch out for the floatplanes!" and I raised a paddle to let her know I heard her.

My shoulders warmed up with the exertion of paddling. The cold water dripped on my hands and arms. After ten minutes I stopped and allowed the boat to drift in the tiny swells. Three ships were in the harbor and floatplanes lined the People's Dock, taking off and landing every half hour, after hauling tourists up over the Mendenhall Glacier. I headed away from the frenetic activity, rather dangerous for a kayaker, and paddled a long way past where I thought the floatplanes would skim the water taking off. I drifted then, lulled by the gentle waves, the grayness of the sky and the water. Even the mountains looked charcoal-gray. Soothing. As the tension in my shoulders melted, my mind emptied—but only for a short while. Images of Magdalena crowded in, Magdalena leaning against David, Magdalena listening quietly in group, Magdalena on the dock with someone. Who could it have been? No witnesses had come forward. She might have been in the wrong place at the wrong time or she might have become a threat to someone. The growing roar of a floatplane behind me broke into my thoughts. It was coming straight for me. I paddled frantically away from it and watched as it lifted right before it reached the spot where I had been drifting in my thoughts. I shook my fist, and the young pilot gave me the finger. So much for the chivalrous image of bush pilots . . .

The telephone was ringing when I walked in the door. Royal's warm voice sent a shiver through me. "Wynne, I just returned from Ka'saan. Will you come up for a drink and help me banish the demons?"

Riding the elevator to the tenth floor gave me time to become really nervous. He opened his door as soon as I rang the doorbell. He pulled me in with a little hug, and my nervousness turned into a protective numbness. I hadn't felt this way about anyone since Jake.

"I am glad to see you, Wynne. I've been taking care of things for Magdalena's family. It's been very hard."

"I'm so sorry, Royal. I hoped you would get the message I left on your answering machine."

He nodded. "I did. It made my day."

We walked through a long hall where both walls were covered with contemporary totemic art. He even had two pieces of David's. In the living room, glass front cabinets and china closets lined cream-colored walls, all of them full of masks and baskets and carved bowls and spoons and halibut hooks. A massive mahogany desk littered with papers occupied the space in front of the windows, which were bare of curtains. From his window I could see clearly how the waters of the Gastineau Channel divided the two masses of land that at one time had held two of the largest gold ore lodes in the world. Now, instead of mining claims, houses stretched out on both sides of the channel, covering the earth that had yielded so many millions of dollars.

Royal glided out of the kitchen carrying on a tray two crystal wineglasses and a bottle of Mouton Cadet. He sat down slowly in a chair close to me. I had to lean back to catch my breath. I felt like a fourteen-year-old being betrayed by my physical reactions. He poured the wine; it only added to the fire already in my stomach. Out of his jacket pocket he pulled a small tissue-wrapped package. Inside lay a delicate pair of porcupine-quill earrings, ten or twelve loops on a side, each loop containing two quills with tiny gold beads at the bottom. "I asked her to make them for me while I was there. And she did as a special favor."

"I *like* them, Royal, I like them very much. With everything that you had to do in Ka'saan, I appreciate your thinking of me."

"I thought of you frequently. It helped me get through the ordeal."

"It must have been rough."

"More than rough." He looked down, remembering. "Her parents kept asking me how such a thing could have happened. They were in shock, of course. Other people in the village, all relatives you know, looked at me accusingly. Their looks plainly said that I should have taken better care of my cousin, that I had been careless, that somehow it was my fault. It was awful. Even my own parents seemed to think that I should have seen something coming and moved to prevent it."

I took a sip of wine before replying. "You've been carrying a double burden, then."

"I couldn't wait to return. I felt guilty about that too."

"Too?"

"I really do feel guilty about Magdalena. I don't know how I could have stopped it. But I do keep wondering if I should have spent more time with her and kept better tabs on what she was doing."

"Been an active big brother?"

"Exactly. I still can't quite believe it. It was a terrible end for anyone. And an ignoble end for one of her caste."

"Her *caste?*"

"In the Tlingit tradition our family is of very high caste and has been for hundreds of years. I suppose, if no whites had ever come, she would have been regarded as a princess."

I was surprised at the way he talked about caste so seriously. Could he have exacted retribution for her living with someone of lower caste? "What would *you* have been?"

"A chief perhaps. Not an art historian." He picked up a beautifully carved rattle and I could picture him using it in a ceremony. The tongue of the main carving, a large green frog, curved into the mouth of a tiny human.

"What is an art historian doing here in Juneau?"

He stood up and walked to the window, still holding the rattle. "Feeding at the public trough. I'm administering a special project for the state, cataloguing the Northwest Coast art objects in private and public collections."

"It must be an enormous project."

"It is. In one way I'm glad, because it means I'll stay in Juneau longer." He turned to look at me.

I ducked my head into my glass. The silence stretched out tautly.

When I lifted my head he still looked at me with his large liquid-brown eyes. "I am also investigating some rumors about the Greenwald."

"You've heard about it too?"

"Too?"

"The night before she died, Magdalena told Ben the Greenwald was being looted. And by someone at the party."

Royal's face was blank. He walked to one of the china closets, which he unlocked with a tiny key and took out a small basket. He placed it on the low table in front of me. "Spruce root. Circa 1860. Made before Lincoln freed the slaves. Woven during the time of Prince Dmitri Masoutov, the last Russian governor of Alaska."

I touched it with one finger, very gently. The weaving was so fine that it reminded me of petit point. A subtle geometric pattern graced the mouth of the basket, and on the top, a tiny lid fit perfectly. Over a hundred years old. "Made by a Tlingit woman?"

"Yes," he said. "I acquired it from a dealer in New York several years ago. It cost a great deal. Of course, it is priceless."

"Was it part of the Greenwald?"

He sat down again next to me. "I think so. Other people, with more knowledge than me, are sure of it. I've been hired by the governor's office to find out. All rather hush-hush, I don't need to tell you."

He drained his glass. "I didn't know Magdalena suspected something. *Could* she have been killed because of it?"

It was a rhetorical question. I went over to the table to put some distance between us. His closeness unnerved me. I wasn't ready for the strong feelings rushing through me. He must have noticed my withdrawal.

"I've been thinking of nothing else since she died, Royal. Why? Who? And I just don't know."

"You're tired. Let's stop thinking about her death for a while. I'll fix you dinner. We'll have salmon stew and pilot bread. I brought back a ton of salmon." He popped into the kitchen. He came back holding out what looked like jerky. "An appetizer, Wynne. Dried salmon. I grew up on it. It tided us over in the winter, when we couldn't catch the fresh fish."

He disappeared again and I could hear him humming and chopping and banging. I felt comatose. It must have been the exertion in the kayak. The rich smell of fish stew was the next thing I remembered. Royal was gently shaking my shoulder. "Here I thought you were communing with my spirit, and I come out to find you asleep."

Sitting at a round pedestal table in the corner, we each downed two large bowls of creamy stew filled with thick chunks of fresh red salmon. I felt better after eating and I said, "I am curious about something, Royal. How do the Tlingit people feel about whites and Natives marrying or even living together?"

He leaned back in his chair, hands behind his head. "I should begin by saying that it is *not* simple. It is one of the many accommodations we have had to make since the whites first came. The same bitterness and resentment and hostility that some feel over the way our home has been claimed spills over into many areas and that is one of them." He rocked back even farther in his chair. "Of course, many years ago, anyone flaunting the marriage taboos was ostracized. And that meant death, because without the help of others they could not live. If an Eagle married an Eagle or a Raven married a Raven, they virtually signed their death warrant. It was an enormous dishonor. And, like the Japanese, 'face' was, and probably still is, very important to us."

I thought for a moment. "Was Magdalena dishonoring her family by living with David?"

"Perhaps 'dishonor' is too strong a word. Let's just say that they hoped she would come to her senses and marry a man they approved of, even if he was not Native."

"They don't care for David?"

"They recognize his superficial nature."

I buttered one last piece of pilot bread, the large round cracker used in place of other bread in bush Alaska. On camping trips the crackers sustained me. Then I slathered them with peanut butter and raspberry jam.

Royal brought a pot of coffee to the table and poured us each a cup. "Now, I have a question for you, Doctor."

I put on my most professional demeanor. "Fire away."

"Was Magdalena mentally ill?"

"You mean in addition to being an alcoholic?"

"Yes."

"I don't know. You have to realize I saw her only in a group setting, and then only three or four times total. I never conducted an examination."

"Sometimes she was so high, sometimes so low." Royal was almost talking to himself.

"Mood swings may indicate the presence of a problem, but the behavior at the top and bottom of each swing has to be erratic and bizarre enough to call it mental illness."

"I never saw her behaving irrationally," he said, "except in choosing to live with David." We both grinned.

From then on we spent an hour chatting aimlessly and I left feeling better than I had since first hearing about Magdalena's death. Sure that her death was connected to the Greenwald, I decided to jump into the fray with Alex and hoped he wouldn't jump me first.

CHAPTER 7

I t was seven o'clock Friday morning when Ben's phone call came. "I realize this is a dreadful hour to call, but this news is too important to wait."

Fully awake with anticipation, I asked, "You talked to Alex?"

"Yes, and I owe you an apology, Wynne. I did stick my head in the sand. Something *is* going on there."

"Did you examine the collection?"

He chuckled, a bass rumble. "Only after a skirmish with Alex."

"It sounds like you enjoyed it."

"I am afraid I did. When I asked to be taken to the rooms where the collection is housed, he treated me as if I were an impertinent tourist off a cruise ship."

"He must have panicked."

"Indeed. I had to remind him I headed the museum board and that he served at our pleasure."

I wiggled with delight at the mental picture. "The big guns."

"Then he had the audacity to tell me his staff couldn't find the catalogue."

The catalogue is the complete listing of the objects in the collection. The museum probably has innumerable copies of such a valuable document. Not being able to "find" the catalogue sounded like a transparent attempt to prevent identification of missing objects. Alex must have been frantic. I wish I had seen his carefully constructed facade crack. The square brown-rimmed glasses, the Brooks Brothers suits, the sticker on his Volvo that proclaimed "I'd rather be sailing" even though he didn't own a sailboat, were all chosen to project the right image.

Ben's excited voice broke into my uncharitable thoughts. "I went down to the basement after I shook off Alex. He was persistent. I couldn't tell without the catalogue, but his behavior was enough to make me suspicious of him."

Got him! With regret, I thought I would rather nail him on sexual harassment. Or murder. Could he have been the one who, threatened by Magdalena's discovery, followed her from the party and threw her off the dock? She had threatened his little empire as well as his carefully erected persona. Before I saw him I wanted to reconnoiter with Rita. My first appointment was at nine o'clock. I shot out of bed, stopping only to pull on something woolly and warm and rainproof, and then briefly at the French bakery for a croissant.

Rita greeted me with strong coffee in a chipped white mug. Her office is very plain. Dirty beige walls and brown industrial carpeting. File cabinets against the walls, papers flowing out of trays, and in the middle of it Rita was sitting behind a large green metal desk. I could sense a difference in her. It was power. It emanated in waves from her. I had felt it when she knelt in my garden, but here in this place of official authority it was almost tangible.

She leaned back in her executive chair. "So how's it going, Wynne? Have you come up with anything?"

I nodded eagerly, tail wagging. I was the junior officer reporting to my commanding officer. "I think her death might be connected in some way to the Greenwald Collection at the museum."

Rita raised her thick black eyebrows in inquiry. I told her about the Greenwald and Magdalena's suspicions and Ben's involvement.

"It sounds as though you might be on the track of something big, but I don't understand how Magdalena could have known that anything was missing. According to you, the collection contains thousands of objects and she worked on it only a few times."

I shrugged. "I don't know. But Alex's behavior with Ben is a tip-off."

"Could Alex have become flustered for any other reason?"

"I suppose having the chair of the board suddenly want to see your biggest collection without warning could have knocked him off balance. But *I* am convinced that he is the one who is selling off the artifacts."

Rita closed her eyes. "I've met Alex. He seems to me to be a jerk. A harmless jerk."

"Not so harmless. He's forced more than one woman off the staff through sexual harassment."

Rita looked at me owlishly. "I had a superior officer who tried that with me once. I told him a story about my family in Italy. They cut off the penis of a man who was bothering one of my female relatives. I described to him all of the details. That officer did not bother me again."

"You make it sound as if sexual harassment is a relatively minor thing."

She waved her hand in dismissal of such a trivial topic. "I think it is a power play. You have to know how to play the game. Many women don't. They feel powerless. Sometimes I lose my patience with them."

"They don't just *feel* powerless, Rita. They *are* powerless."

She held out her hands, palms up. "We can't agree on this, Wynne. But now is the time to question Alex."

I sat up straighter in my chair. "Let me at him!"

"I'm sorry, Wynne. I don't think it's appropriate that you be the one to question him."

"Give me a break. I want to see him squirm."

"That's the problem. You are too preoccupied with this issue of sexual harassment and your own hostile feelings toward him. Anger clouds thinking."

I slumped back as much as it is possible to slump in a metal office chair and considered what she said. She was right. I can't stand Alex. "I'm a trained psychologist,

Rita. I learned to suspend judgment, not to let my feelings spill into an interview." I pulled out my trump card. "And anyway, Alex has always had a thing for me. He might be less guarded with me than with a police officer."

She pursed her lips, staring above my head. I held my breath while the silence lengthened.

"Okay, Wynne. You can do it. Call me after you talk to him."

The day dragged for me. Once I arranged to meet with Alex after work at his house I found myself continually looking at the clock.

It still drizzled as I made my way toward his house. The foliage of all the wild plants drooped with the weight of the rain. I shook droplets off my anorak like a dog as I stood on his porch ringing the bell. He opened it wide while motioning me in with a big, unsuspecting grin on his puss. The living room screamed Scandinavian. Smooth blond wood furniture, Marimekko prints on square cushions, simple wood sculptures, bare expanses of white wall punctuated with metal-framed prints, rag rugs on polished pine floors, and curtainless windows. Alex poured coffee for us into pottery mugs. Naturally.

We sat on the couch. Alex widened his large spaniel eyes at me, preparatory to making a pass. "I always wanted to get to know you better, Wynne. What a beautiful sweater you're wearing. It matches your eyes."

His next move would bring him much closer to me. I could feel him preparing to spring. "You're sweet." I almost gagged as I said this. "I need your help, Alex. You were Magdalena's boss. Did you notice anything about her behavior at work that was different?"

Taken aback, he straightened quickly. "Magdalena? Surely others could tell you more. She was just a receptionist. In the normal course of things I had very little to do with her. What business is it of *yours* anyway, Wynne?"

I looked down at my hands and twisted them a bit and tried to squeeze a tear out. "She was a very special client of mine and I made a promise to someone close to her to find out what really happened. It was such a shock."

"It was, I suppose, but nothing to do with me."

"Why do you say that?"

"I figure she ended up in the wrong place at the wrong time. Some pretty rough characters hang out on the dock at night."

I was not convinced, but I only shrugged. "Perhaps. You know"—and here I looked directly at him, not accusingly—"she talked a great deal about the museum to me and to other people. She was particularly interested in the Greenwald."

He started at the mention of the Greenwald and sipped his coffee to hide his emotion. "I don't know why. She had no more contact with it than any person outside the museum did."

"I understand she worked on it twice."

He rubbed his dark mustache until I was sure it would rub off. "I don't really know, Wynne."

Liar. "Perhaps you could tell me about her last days."

"I really hate to disappoint you, Wynne, but nothing out of the ordinary happened. She came to work at eight, manned the reception desk—oops, I should say, wom-anned the reception desk—and then went home at four-thirty, like everyone else. I didn't really have much to do with her. I'm usually upstairs in my office." He looked at his watch, crusted with gold nuggets. "I *must* go, Wynne. Some business for the museum."

I made no move to leave. "I've been wondering about the connection between your party and her death. She *was* murdered when she left here."

He waved a hand airily. "Sheer coincidence, Wynne."

"I wonder."

"I really don't like your tone, Wynne."

He overused "really." I suppose liars feel compelled to say "really" and "truly" and "frankly." "But you see how it looks, Alex. She goes to your party, leaves alone. The only ones who know where she is are those at the party. Anyone could have followed her from there and no one else would have noticed. Even *you* could have done it."

"That's *it*, Wynne! You've gone too far. Practically accusing me in my own house . . ." He was sputtering. "The only time I left was to talk to one of the girls—I mean women—in the garden."

"She had a secret, Alex. She discovered someone was looting the Greenwald. She told Ben at your party. And then she died."

His face became a vicious mask. "Well, she was a liar and a sneak. Get *out*, Wynne."

He slammed the door in my face. I felt shaky after that encounter and suspected that Rita would not be pleased about my performance. Feeling as if I'd bungled the questioning, I walked downtown aimlessly. The misty rain soaked through my parka. It was time to seal the seams again. I didn't know much more than when I started. Honky-tonk piano music tinkled out of the Red Dog Saloon. I pushed through the swinging wooden doors and sat on a high stool at the bar and ordered a beer from the smiling bartender. What a ghastly job he had. To smile at customers all day and put up with the same questions from drunken tourists. Having just walked off a cruise ship anchored at the dock, they would ask what elevation Juneau is. Sure, I felt sorry for the bartender, but sorrier for myself. I *had* botched it. Really. Now Alex was alerted to my suspicions. I wondered if he had covered himself in the Greenwald matter. Probably not very well. Nobody could prove he had left the party either. Everyone was too drunk to notice anything. I called Rita from the dirty pay phone in the corner and told her the gist of the conversation. She didn't sound as disappointed as I felt. Maybe she didn't expect much. She invited me for dinner for Saturday evening. I agreed halfheartedly.

Another beer waited for me on the polished wood bar when I returned to my stool. A man I knew slightly, Kevin, raised his glass to me. What's the old saying? What the hell, might as well. A fishing guide for rich tourists, he was in port for one night and would be taking out another charter in the morning. We reeled from one bar to another, with more and more people joining us, until the group had swelled to fifteen or so. We listened to music at the Red Dog, played pool at the New York, ate hot dogs at the Triangle, and danced at the Penthouse. We all parted amicably at about three or so, some to beds together, others to solitary beds. I stumbled home alone, having decided that I didn't really like Kevin all that much, who, by that time, was falling-down drunk anyway.

*　　　*　　　*

I slept until noon on Saturday and woke up without a
hangover, thanks to the two aspirin I took the night before. I picked at my invalid's meal of dry toast and tea
(can't be too careful after a night of boozing—at least I
had the sense to stay away from tequila chasers) and listened to Vivaldi on the radio. Guilt must have propelled
me into a thorough housecleaning, which lasted until it
was time to dress for dinner. I took some care, ironing a
silk double-breasted blouse and a flaring trumpet skirt,
both in rich shades of brown. I even added more auburn
highlights to my hair and polished my nails with an
opaque tint. On the way over to Rita's, I noticed the rasp-
berries were ripe near her house. I looked around for a
container, even a piece of litter would do, but nothing
sprang to the eye. Rita greeted me in a navy blue silk
dress, with a white lace collar on her wide shoulders. She
also wore an apron. Mom. The powerful police detective
lurked beneath that apron. She looked out the door at the
luxuriant hillside. "The kids are somewhere picking rasp-
berries for dessert. Come back into the kitchen."

We walked through the living room, where the furniture was covered with a sturdy-looking brown plaid fab-
ric and the only picture on the wall was a blown-up
photograph of her children in their best clothes grinning
toothily at the camera. The kitchen was a duplicate of
hundreds throughout Juneau. White walls, orange Formica countertops, and dark wood cabinets. On a tall coun-
tertop in the middle, she'd been rolling out dough. She
gestured toward it. "I always make my own noodles. I hate

the packaged kind. No taste, no texture. Like rubber bands." She filled a glass with red wine from a gaily colored pottery jug and handed it to me. "Peasant wine. It reminds me of my roots. Harsh but warming." It burned going down, but the warmth spread quickly in a very agreeable way. She shook out a cigarette, looked around furtively before lighting it, and blew the smoke out the window over the sink. "So, how'd it go with Alex?"

I dreaded her question. I shrugged and sat down on a stool. "He finally told me to get out after I pressed him about the Greenwald. *That* I know he's guilty of. Magdalena's murder is another story. He did call her a liar and a sneak. He admitted leaving the party once. But as he said, and others corroborate, everyone was too drunk to notice anything."

Rita nodded. "Motive?"

"He could have killed her to silence her about the Greenwald. To a man like Alex status and prestige are everything. He would be stripped of both if he were even *accused* of stealing." As I talked about it, another thought came unbidden into my mind. "What if Magdalena were not innocent in all of this? What if she threatened to blackmail Alex? She could have forced him to choose David's work for the Smithsonian show." I took another sip of the wine. I was sure it was helping me to think. "Even though that isn't a great deal to do—certainly David's work does belong in that show—but Alex wouldn't know when the blackmail might stop. I think he could kill someone to prevent his secret from leaking."

Rita pushed out her lower lip. "Good reasoning, Wynne." I felt as if I had passed a crucial exam. I glowed.

Rita stubbed out her cigarette and began cutting the noodles into thin strips. "I'm making a cream sauce for these noodles, Wynne. Sinfully rich." She glanced at me. "Now, for our next suspect. David."

"I know those near and dear are always suspected first, but I can't see what killing Magdalena would gain for *him*."

"You want motives?" Rita ticked them off on her floury fingertips. "Money, jealousy, fear, anger, freedom, gain of some sort. On the face of it David is on top—his work is commanding high prices, and he is considered to be a real comer in the art world. And he had a beautiful and intelligent companion."

"Who he says inspired his recent work, much of which is based on Tlingit myth and legend. It would be killing the goose who lays the golden eggs."

Rita stirred the cream sauce slowly. "Perhaps she demanded too much of him. Perhaps she was jealous of his new fame."

"That doesn't sound like her." Something bothered me. What was it that Tyler had said? "Tyler complained about Magdalena lately. Apparently David told him that he couldn't do as much work as before because of Magdalena, that somehow her problems came before his paintings. I do know Tyler was very hot about that. As a motive it seems rather trivial."

Rita laughed, a harsh little bark. "Trivial! People will kill for a dime, they'll kill because someone gives them a dirty look, they'll kill just because they feel like it. Just because they can. People are the most vicious animals on earth. That's why we need God."

Sobering thought. I waved at the kids out the window. They held up their baskets, which looked almost full, and then ran back into the woods, where the weeds grew above their heads.

Rita lit another cigarette, and she, too, glanced out the window as she did so. "Let's go on. Our next suspect is Royal."

"But we have absolutely no evidence that they had any kind of relationship other than the kinship one." The wine must have gone to my head, for I found myself flushing. "I really think we can eliminate him, Rita." I enunciated very clearly. "He has no motive."

She poured me some more wine before saying, "He could have any number of motives, Wynne. The honor of the family. Greed. She might have possession of some family artifacts. Blackmail. They may have been working together. A falling out among thieves. One of the most charming men I ever met did away with a number of women in a particularly grisly way."

I could see she was about to describe the way he killed them. I waved a white dish towel in surrender. "Okay, okay. Leave me some appetite for those noodles."

Just then the children walked in, swinging their buckets and sniffing the air suspiciously. Rita must have disposed of the cigarette in the sink behind her as she smiled at them artlessly. What parents have to put up with from their kids!

While we dined on fettuccine Alfredo, a lightly dressed green salad, and crusty Italian bread, the children regaled us with tales of Little League, where the adults act like children and the children act like adults. Rita listened as attentively to them as she did to me, talking only when she told a story in which her kids starred. She pressed food on all of us and then, when I couldn't swallow another bite, brought in raspberry shortcake piled high with whipped cream. After dessert the children excused themselves and barreled outside again, where it was broad daylight even though the clock had just struck nine.

Rita and I each settled into an easy chair, with tiny glasses of amaretto. I could barely keep my eyes open but wanted to fill her in on different conversations I had with Tyler and Sonja and Greta and Ben. When I finished she sat for a long time, fingering her glass, her lace-covered bosom rising and falling slowly. "All of your work, Wynne, creates a good context for the crime but still sheds no light on the killer." I thought I had come up with several good motives, and said so. "We are speculating, Wynne. What we need is a witness."

Almost a week later I presented her with one.

CHAPTER 8

All week long the rain came out of the sky in strings—no breaks between the drops. My mood soon matched the weather. Gray and gloomy. It seemed as though every crazy in Juneau was coming to the attention of officialdom, who required a mental status for each of them from *me*. I saw little of Jane, who was working very hard on the child sexual-abuse case involving the minister. Whenever I saw her she smiled abstractedly, hands full of paper, and kept moving. Magdalena slid to the back of my mind and popped up infrequently and I got to the stage where I was planning a reorganization of my closets and actually looking forward to it. A very low period.

Thursday afternoon all that changed. I heard Joe before I saw him. He sang, "Give me that old soft shoe . . ." as he sailed through the reception room and my open door. He stopped a few feet from my desk and stood, grinning, hat angled rakishly. The hat! It was an unbelievable piece of kitsch. He turned slowly to give me the full benefit of his artistry. Originally a cowboy hat, Joe had covered it with political buttons, playing cards, plastic swizzle sticks, crumpled gum wrappers, bar napkins, ceramic pins of salmon and bear and moose, pigeon feathers and one long eagle feather, and raisins spray-painted gold to look like gold nuggets. It stunned the viewer. Joe bowed before me, then lowered himself into the rocker and flipped out a cigarette. I passed him a match and an ashtray and he leaned back, taking care that the hat was still posed in the best position.

"I can see you like it." He blew smoke toward me.

"It is fantastic." "Like" is such a relative word, isn't it?

"So do the tourists." He looked mighty pleased with himself.

"I'll bet they try to buy an old character like you drinks."

He grinned. "And smokes too. I've got to beat them off."

"Quite a racket."

"Yeah." He leaned forward with a solemn look on his face. "Only thing is, each one of them wants to put something on the hat. It's getting too heavy to wear. Tires me out when I'm doing the Watusi with the young ones."

"I'll bet you *never* go to bed."

He winked. "Not before the bars close. You never know what might turn up."

Old rascal. "I suppose you weren't around when Magdalena Peratravitch was killed?"

"Naw." He stubbed the cigarette out and lit another. I should have known. What did I expect? Joe wasn't really a client. I don't know if he ever had been. My clients want to change. He doesn't. He is perfectly happy with his life. Or, at least he says he is. It must get tough for a sixty-year-old man to live in a crummy room on peanut butter sandwiches. Until he was thirty he was a brilliant but erratic engineer with a wife and three daughters. Then he started having the wide mood swings and bizarre episodes characteristic of a manic-depressive disorder. I met him when he was fifty, just out of jail for some piece of mischief, supposedly taking his lithium daily. I was supposed to monitor him. It was like monitoring an earthquake. All I could do was watch him. I couldn't make him take his meds. Since then he drops in to chat once in a while. I bring him canned goods and visit him in jail.

I sighed. The rain pressed in on me.

His voice came through the fog of my consciousness. "I know a guy who *was* there. He was scared to death until the police quit coming around."

"You mean he didn't tell them?"

"Hell, no!" Joe looked at me incredulously. Why help out the enemy?

"This friend of yours," I proceeded slowly, "he actually saw something?"

Joe nodded. "He was having a little drink by himself squeezed in between two buildings. He shook real bad for a week after he saw it."

"What was it that he saw?"

"That gal getting killed! What do you think?"

My excitement bubbled up. "Do you think he'd talk to me about it?"

"Why?"

Good question. I looked down at my hands. "She was a client of mine. I want to find out who killed her. It means a lot to me."

"I'll try to set it up. But no cops!"

After he sauntered out the door, hat perched proudly, I sat for a few minutes, relishing the knowledge that I might have an eyewitness that the police had missed. It wasn't a noble feeling, but I enjoyed it just the same. It lasted through the next four hours when I conducted a court-ordered examination of a young woman who was recognized as truly psychotic by everyone. Even a young child could tell that something was terribly wrong with her. She sat rigidly in the chair, face immobile, hands twisting ceaselessly as she spoke in a mechanical monotone about the people who were after her. Self-inflicted cigarette burns dotted her arms and hands. I prayed she wouldn't get pregnant until I completed a report since I was recommending treatment in a closed facility. I questioned if she could *really* be treated anywhere successfully.

After I printed the report I wandered into Jane's office, where books and papers littered the landscape, covering her old oak desk, her battered file cabinet, and her two bookcases. The contrast between her scrupulously clean house and her messy office usually set off a train of thought about her real feelings about her work that I had never, ever revealed to her. She looked up, and, in a characteristic movement, twisted her hair away from her face and jabbed a few pins into it.

"We are about ready to go to court, Wynne. I even found two more little girls who will testify. This guy got around to quite a few of the kids in his congregation."

"Horrifying."

"Normal. It is most often the guys in some position of authority. Kids are used to obeying, particularly those who are perceived as powerful. If I could say one thing to parents about child sexual abuse I would say—teach your children to question all authority."

"Many parents interpret that to mean rearing sassy kids."

"Better sassy ones than victimized ones."

"I suppose. Say, how about a drink? There's a new piano player at the Baranof."

"I'd love to, Wynne, but I can't. I want to finish this and then I have an interview after dinner."

I felt a big letdown and realized how much I wanted her company. "How about dinner then?"

She looked at me hard, her whole demeanor almost vibrating with energy. "Okay. How about Ozawa's?" She looked at her big L. L. Bean watch. "I'll meet you there in an hour and a half."

I had time to catch an aerobics class at the exercise studio. I grabbed a leotard from my office closet and ran over for the after-work class, usually full to bursting with the less-than-conscientious types, the ones who wake up too late for the early-bird class, the ones who eat a Danish at midmorning break, French fries for lunch, and then get an attack of the guilts at about 3:30, and arrive at the after-work class slightly late with virtuous looks on their faces.

I'm one of them too. We bent and twisted and kicked together while observing ourselves sweat in a ten-by-forty-foot mirror. Most wore matching tights and leotards, state-of-the-art exercise togs, one of the more visible results of a bulging oil-rich economy. Maybe the oil money did make us into blue-eyed Arabs, buying without conscience and, many would say, without taste and restraint. After the grand finale and cool-down, I took a shower, and walked down to the café, where Jane was already waiting, trading wisecracks with the proprietor, whose menu reflected his origins. Hamburgers and French fries alongside ramen and fried rice.

After I ordered Asian noodles I was still thinking about how the oil money changed Alaska. We sat at the counter and watched Harry try to burn the hands of his regulars while he refilled coffee cups. A few yelped and then grinned sheepishly at having been caught by the old trick. Every man in the place wore a baseball cap, and even some of the women did.

I turned to Jane. She was engrossed in a byplay between Harry and one of his customers, who were arguing about whether the city government was any damn good. "Do you think the money changed Alaska a great deal?"

"Lord, yes." She laughed at some vulgar witticism of Harry's. "When I was growing up here it seemed like everyone was in the same boat. Not much money, wedded to the outdoors, nuts about fishing and hunting and boating, and to hell with the Joneses." She shook her fist at a customer who was making disparaging remarks about women drivers. I couldn't see how she could track so many conversations. "Now, some wet-behind-the-ears jerk from Outside barely out of law school can pull down eighty grand a year, buy tailor-made clothes in New York, Oriental rugs for his cabin, and an enormous boat that he can afford to keep in a slip all year even though he takes it out only once. And then he has the nerve to call himself a real Alaskan, just because he lives here."

I noticed that whenever Jane is in a certain environment, these attitudes about old-timers and newcomers emerge. And now she had an audience. Some guy in a dark red halibut jacket prepared to speak by pointing his finger. "And they don't know a damn thing about Alaska. They read about it, all right, and they're even living here, but they don't know jackshit about the country."

Jane nodded vigorously. "The way I see it, Bill, is that the boomers will go home when it's all over and leave us to clean up the mess."

"Damn straight. Those Ay-rabs in OPEC will start cutting each other's throats soon and the bottom will drop out of the oil market and we'll be left high and dry. Then Mr. and Mrs. Fancy-pants will hightail it back to wherever they came from. And good riddance to them." Bill drained his coffee cup, left his money on the counter, waved to everybody, and left.

I turned to Jane. "Sounds like you're stirring up trouble."

"Trouble's been here all along, Wynne. The land-of-opportunity business is all true and I think that is why most people come. But easy money undercuts values like hard work and betrays those people who have lived here a long time. They fished or hunted or maybe just built up a life for themselves over a long period of time working hard, every year getting a little bit further ahead, but always with the awareness that Alaska can be brutal. Then the money started flowing in. People began making tons of money, mostly people who have just moved to Alaska, mostly people who are young and unencumbered, and then they spend very conspicuously. At the same time, they are flexing political muscles and throwing their weight around. It's a bitter pill for the old-timers to swallow."

"What about the Natives?"

"I think the general prosperity has affected them, too, but the kids are still dropping out of high school and the adults are still in the lower-level jobs and cultural pride is still mighty slow in coming."

Harry brought our order, enormous bowls of steaming noodles topped with chicken chunks and egg slices and chopped green onions. We dumped soy sauce in and started slurping.

Jane looked up from her bowl. "And for some reason we seem to have more and more homeless people. How can that be when we have so much money?"

We could look out the window of the café and see men hanging out on the street, worn-out men, waiting for the Glory Hole to open so that they could get a hot meal.

Harry gestured angrily toward them. "They could work. I need a dishwasher. Think any of them will take the job? No. All they want to do is drink. As long as the Glory Hole is open, they'll keep drinking. No reason for them to quit." He stomped back into the kitchen.

"That's true enough of Joe. He'll never quit. He came to see me today, Jane. He says he knows someone"—and here I lowered my voice—"who saw Magdalena get killed."

"You're obsessed by her murder, Wynne. It worries me that you're involved."

"You're obsessed by your preacher who goes after little girls. I don't tell *you* to leave it alone."

"It's not dangerous, Wynne. Not like going after a murderer."

"Not dangerous? What about the man who threatened your life after you exposed him? What about the woman who tried to throttle you in the courtroom after you accused her husband of sexually abusing her daughter? What about the guy that pulled the gun? You've got a lot of nerve."

Jane had the grace to look sheepish. "You're right, I guess. Violence is violence, whether it is child sexual abuse or murder."

Harry heard her say "sexual abuse" and he leaned over the counter, hands flat. His slanted brown eyes widened. "They ought to string those guys up, Jane, or at least make sure they can never use it again." He made a slashing movement at his pelvis. He picked up the glass pot and refilled our coffee cups. "I heard you talk. You don't get that guy, you tell me. I'll make sure he gets what he deserves."

Jane nodded solemnly at Harry, who walked back to the kitchen. "I wish it were that easy. They used to blue-ticket undesirables out of town. No punishment, just banishment. But I really want to put this guy away for a long time." She looked at her watch. "Got to go, Wynne. Good luck with your sleuthing. I mean it."

Harry, toothpick twirling, came out when Jane left. "I

like that kid. Her dad used to bring her in here from the time she was little. He was a highliner, best fisherman in the fleet."

"You see a lot in this business, don't you?"

He looked at me appraisingly. "Yeah. What are you interested in?" Harry was sharp.

"Magdalena Peratravitch's murder."

"That girl." He shook his head sadly. "She used to come in with her cousin. They argued sometimes, I think about her living with that white guy."

Swell. They used to argue in a public place. A place known for gossip and tittle-tattle. I hadn't wanted to hear that. "Big arguments?"

"Naw. It was sort of chronic with them. They'd talk about pictures and family and sometimes they'd argue about her boyfriend. I never seen the boyfriend."

I woke early after a restless night. A storm had lashed the house all night, the wind a counterpoint to my nightmares. Only a few scraps of fog remained in the morning. Outside, everything, the flowers, the path, the stairs, even the buildings downtown looked scrubbed clean. Raindrops still trembled on the foliage. Even though the day looked special, I dragged to work. I was no further with my investigation and I was beginning to feel as if nothing matters in the long run. You know the feeling. You start thinking about the universe, the stars, the millions of lives that have preceded you, and wonder why you struggle on when it really doesn't make any difference in the scheme of things. I hate that mood. I thought of playing hooky but nothing interested me. I live in one of the biggest natural playgrounds in the world and nothing drew me—not mountain, not beach, not sea, not rain forest.

My first client of the day was waiting for me. It was a man who was impotent and, quite naturally, depressed about it. I referred him to the psychiatrist, who could prescribe an antidepressant for him and then told him, as gently as I could, that no one in Juneau, including myself, knew much about sexual problems. I recommended that he try a clinic down south and gave him a list of them. Poor guy. Impotence is the devil to treat. It's all tied up with self-image and childhood experiences and parental attitudes. How can you go back and undo how you were physically handled as a child? The body has to be handled respectfully and happily from the time a baby is born if good sexual attitudes are to be engendered.

My sour mood changed when Joe walked in, almost furtively. "He'll talk to you, Wynne." Joe spoke softly out of the side of his mouth. "Meet us at the Golden Garter after work." He sidled out.

At 4:30 I raced down the hill, so eager that I had to force myself to slow down and not overwhelm the old geezer. A ship was in and the passengers filled the streets. Why do cruise passengers always buy whites for a trip? And navy blue? And red? They were so easy to spot. If they weren't decked out in red, white, and blue, then they were wearing the cheap see-through plastic raincoats. Even though I sauntered rather than loped, I reached the bar in record time. My eyes took a moment to adjust to the dim interior after the dazzle of the sun. It was beginning to fill up, the braver tourists venturing in for a taste of the real Alaska. Ever since Jack London, the archetype of the Alaskan bar contains certain elements: crossed snowshoes on the walls, oil-lamp fixtures with glass chimneys, stuffed animal heads peering into the dark interior, bear and beaver and caribou skins stretched on the rough board walls, heavy mahogany bars with footrests, and sawdust floors. The Golden Garter was no exception. Joe lounged at a table in the back, alone. My heart plummeted.

Seeing my face, he said, "He'll be here, don't worry. Relax and buy me a drink."

"And contribute to your disreputable behavior?" I walked to the long bar, which looked as if it had been there since the turn of the century, and ordered two coffees.

The bartender scowled as he passed them to me.

Joe and I sipped coffee until an old man slipped into a chair next to us. I hadn't even seen him come through the door. He tipped his hat to me as Joe introduced us. Tommy could have been fifty, but he looked eighty. One of those down-and-outers who keep descending. He wore a greasy wool felt hat pulled down over dirty gray hair, a torn plaid shirt, and old jeans a bit too short for him. He slumped in his chair and flicked his eyes over the room quickly and furtively. Compared to him, Joe was a healthy, lively specimen.

"I want a whiskey," he whispered.

Joe gave me a dirty look as I got up to get him one. The bartender didn't scowl when he handed it to me, so I did. It gave me childish pleasure.

Tommy grabbed the glass as if it were his only friend and didn't let go during the whole interview. He sipped cautiously. His face began to show some signs of life.

"I'm interested in what you saw the night Magdalena Peratravitch died," I said.

"I didn't know who it was I seen until the police came." His eyes looked very moist.

"Can you tell me what happened?"

He looked at Joe for final confirmation that I was all right. Joe nodded. "It was like this, see. I was having a little drink by myself up there across from the dock." He pointed in the general direction of where the murder had occurred. "It was dark and I was sitting in between two buildings. All of a sudden I heard people yelling. I got scared and squeezed back in further."

I noticed his hands were trembling. "Could you see anything?"

"Not right away. Then I saw two people on the dock. They was fighting."

"Physically fighting?"

"Naw. Just yelling at each other."

"Could you hear what they said?"

He shook his head. "I was too far away. All I could hear was yelling."

Both Joe and I kept silent, not wanting to interrupt the flow of words that was coming faster and faster.

"I wasn't going to get involved, no sir. Good way to get killed. Man and woman fighting. Anyway, it happens all the time. They get tanked up and start fighting. He slaps her around a little and then they go away."

The dark underbelly of Juneau sounded inhuman. A place where helping someone could get you hurt. It sounded too much like New York City, a place every Juneauite believed to be hell on earth, Los Angeles running a close second.

"But then, then he grabbed her around the neck and he was swinging her around, God, it was awful." He gulped down his drink. "I want another."

I ran and fetched another one for him, fearful that he would stop talking.

He gulped a mouthful of his new drink. "I didn't know what to do. I was so scared. It looked like he was killing her. I could still hear her though. She was gagging. Then he threw her over the edge. Just like that. She was gone." Tommy was crying now, large tears running down his seamed cheeks. He wiped them with his ragged sleeves and grabbed his glass again.

"Then what happened, Tommy?" Joe was caught up in the story too.

Tommy shrugged. "He just sat there on the edge for a little while. Just sat there. Then he walked uptown."

Tommy gazed off in the distance, reliving that night. "I didn't move till morning. I guess I went to sleep there."

"Do you think you could recognize the man, Tommy?"

"I never seen his face close up. He was tall and dark and kinda skinny. That's all I know."

"Could you tell what his hair looked like? His clothing?"

His eyes were beginning to go blank. "I couldn't see nothing."

Nothing but a murder.

❋   ❋   ❋

Rita didn't look impressed when I told her about Tommy. "Notoriously unreliable eyewitnesses, Wynne. And he was across the street from where it happened."

"If they're so unreliable, how come you questioned every wino in town after the murder?"

"Routine."

Routine, ha! She felt chagrin because I had turned up a witness. Me. An amateur. "Give me a break, Rita. I found an eyewitness to the crime, someone your boys couldn't locate."

She stood up and poured us some more wine from her pottery jug. "Okay, okay. It is something. But we can't give his description much weight."

"Why not?"

"He was too far away and he was drinking and his brain cells are nonexistent."

I sipped my wine cautiously. A rich golden red, it relaxed me too quickly. Rita noticed my tentative approach. "My relatives made it and sent me a case. How do you like it?"

"It's quite potent."

"You psychologists. Always holding something back. Do you like it?"

"Yes, I like it, but it's too fast-acting."

"I have the solution for you." She turned to the stove purposefully and turned back to me with a plateful of pasta. "Eat. We had an early supper because the kids went to the first showing of the movie. Plenty left over."

Spicy bits of Italian sausage in a red sauce topped the rigatoni. I inhaled it. And then regretted it. Rita stood over me with a satisfied smile on her face, saying nothing.

She was just fattening up the calf. I could feel it. I tried to be noncommittal. "New recipe, Rita?"

"Old one. Old family recipe. You loved it, didn't you?"

"Oh, it was good." I didn't want to be too enthusiastic. Caution.

"You're holding back again. What's the matter, are you afraid I'll ask to borrow money or something?"

I had to laugh. "It's the 'something' that bothers me. Even though you won't credit it, Tommy says our killer is tall and dark and slim. Alex and David are tall and dark and slim. So is Royal. I'm afraid he's still in the running in your mind and I don't want to get so relaxed that I can't defend him."

"You've got it bad, don't you?"

"I have to admit it. Yes. I do. Therefore he couldn't be a murderer, no matter what anyone says." I knew my face was getting red. Despite my best efforts I had drained the glass and Rita had filled it again. I was remembering what Harry had said about Magdalena and Royal arguing. I had to tell her. I guess that's why I tried unsuccessfully to resist her wine and pasta. Maybe I had some idea about holding back. But I knew I couldn't. We had made a deal to work together. I spilled it.

A small frown appeared between her bushy black eyebrows. She lit a cigarette with the furtiveness of the ex-addict. Tapping her broad fingers on the counter absently, she blew smoke out the window over the sink.

"By itself, it isn't significant, Wynne. People in families argue all the time. But we do have to consider it in light of what happened. It might have been a very long-standing quarrel between them that just erupted one night." She blew more smoke out in a long thin stream of gray. "Sorry, Wynne, he's still in the running."

I walked to the shore of Gold Creek without noticing where I headed. It soothed me to sit on the granite boulders and watch, with eyes slightly unfocused, the water tumbling from the mountain. Gold Creek is not a misnomer. In fact, few creeks in the area lack gold. Tiny granules and flakes of gold are washed down every year into little pockets. Anyone can swirl a gold pan and show color. It was to this creek that Kowee, the Tlingit chief, directed Juneau and Harris, two disreputable prospectors. Was it a gesture of friendship, this sharing of wealth, or a wish for change, or a way to help his own people? He surely knew what would happen. The white people would start coming and never stop. Too many of them. Us. Maybe Kowee believed the Americans would be an improvement on the Russians. By that time most of the Russians were gone, having decimated the gentle seagoing Aleuts by using them as slave labor to hunt the sea otter, which they also decimated. The fierce Tlingits they had left alone. Maybe Kowee saw the opportunity to bring his people into the nineteenth century. Maybe he just wanted more guns. Whatever his goals, once the gold was discovered, the trickle of people turned into a flow. By the time of the Klondike gold rush in 1897, Juneau was an established, smug little community with several newspapers, hotels, an opera house, a number of small stamp mills, and two large working gold mines. And where were the Tlingits in the midst of this bustle of white middle-class upwardly-mobile activity? Around the edges, I would guess. They moved into town slowly to work in the canneries, living on the beach in their enormous longhouses, prey to alcoholism and consumption, gradually submerging their Indian identities. Now they were trying to reclaim it. Personally, I think it is too late. I don't think I will tell Royal that. After almost one hundred years of having white values shoved down their throats, the Tlingits must feel tremendous frustration and even rage. After all, they were once the rulers here. Everyone was terrified of them. Their ferocity was legendary. They killed with impunity. I didn't like where my thoughts were heading, so I jerked them away from an appraisal of Royal as a killer and thought instead about walking home the long way through the woods.

CHAPTER 9

"Wynne, do come with me. We'll have fun," Michael's voice wheedled over the phone.

"I hate auctions, Michael. I find them very unsettling." Others find them exciting. All I know is that they make me feel a little sick.

"All of your suspects will be there. Please. I'll be bored stiff without you and I must write something about the damn thing."

I caved in. The crack about my "suspects" did it. "For you, Michael, only for you."

"You're a brick, Wynne. Let me fix dinner for you before we go."

"Sure, I'll chance it."

* * *

Michael's cooking reflected his erratic personality. Once he had presented me with water so that we could experience hunger. Another time he concocted very small portions of different foods so that we could really taste each one by keeping it in our mouths for a long, long time. I braced myself mentally before each dining occasion with him.

Royal had called midweek and asked to join us at the auction. My heart went pitty-pat as I agreed. I looked forward to seeing the two of them together.

Michael opened the door to his tiny ground-floor apartment wearing a white chef's apron and puffed hat. I sniffed the air cautiously. It smelled like unusual food, with a sweet and spicy odor. Feeling relief that I would be fed, after all, I slung myself onto one of his built-in padded benches and watched him poke and prod and stir our dinner. I could see him easily in the kitchen because he lived in one room of a large old house. He actually owned the whole house but rented out the rest. Not for him the rich leathery browns and creams and dark reds aspired to by those men who wished to be thought of as "gentlemen." Instead, it seemed as if he had deliberately chosen the antithesis of those shades—bright yellow careened into brilliant orange on top of turquoise and jade green. I never found it jarring, but neither did I find it soothing. Like Michael, it was unexpected and fun. Very little freestanding furniture cluttered the room. When he first considered living in one room he was in a minimalist mood, deciding that furniture was nothing but a bother. He built sturdy shelves, the narrow ones for his books and objects, the medium widths for his stereo and VCR and computer, and wide shelves for benches and beds. Cushions and pillows were invitingly placed nearly every-where and Afghani tribal rugs in deep reds covered the floor. In front of me on a folding oak snack table Michael reverently placed a glass of wine.

"Lord, Michael, don't make me *appreciate* wine tonight. I just want to *drink* the stuff."

He waved a wooden spoon at me reprovingly. "You are a barbarian, Wynne, and I am trying very hard to educate your palate."

I could see that arguing would only prolong my "lesson," so I acquiesced as gracefully as possible.

"Now, take a very small sip, roll it around on your tongue, make sure it reaches every place in your mouth. Only then may you swallow it."

I rolled, taking pains to notice the taste. A ruby red color; I thought it tasted a bit smoky. Now was the hard part of my "lesson." I had to describe it. "It has a nutty nose."

Michael jumped up and down. "It does *not* have a nutty nose, Wynne. You read that in some wine magazine and you say it about every wine I present you with. I give up."

He always said that, too, until the next time. Now I could really drink the stuff. "Hope you have another bot-tle."

"At fifty bucks a crack? You must be joking!"

"Why do you *do* this to me, Michael? You know it's wasted on me. Well, almost. I do appreciate it. But surely you could share a bottle with a knowledgeable friend . . ."

"It is the Dr. Dolittle instinct in me. My wine friends would not tolerate my pompous manner."

I leaned back on a turquoise cushion and sipped. On an easel leaned a painting, unframed, just the canvas. Tiny dots of color had been applied painstakingly to create a sweeping image of beach, water, mountain, and wildflowers. "Who is the pointillist?"

"Woman in Sitka. Rather fine work, isn't it?" He didn't wait for me to answer. "The detail is incredible. Her feeling for nature comes through."

"What feeling for nature?"

Michael smiled lopsidedly. "The whole composition is structured to show how those wildflowers, which are the focal point, grow as a result of the rain from the mountainside, the sun bouncing off the water, and the fertilization of the seaweed."

"Michael, that sounds like another kind of fertilizer."

He clasped his hands together, laughing, the chef's hat falling off his head. "I've spent years studying art and artists. The ones with integrity, the ones not corrupted by the marketplace, express their life philosophies in their work. Their feelings, their beliefs, come through clearly. Jake did it, Wynne."

"How can you say that, Michael? He just painted . . . well, he painted all *sorts* of different things."

"Did you ever notice how somber his work was, how heavy, how burdened, how fateful?" He came and sat beside me to make sure that I wasn't crying. His movement reminded me of the many hours I'd spent in this room with him, both of us crying, our arms around each other. "No matter what he painted, whether it was the sea in a storm or Juneau with the mountain looming over it, a sense of darkness prevailed."

"It is true, what you say. His paintings *are* gloomy. I suppose I didn't want to see it. They were becoming gloomier."

Michael hugged me. Then he continued to speak from the kitchen area as he put the food on our plates. "I can discern the soul of an artist by studying the work."

I shook my head. I thought it was just more hyperbole. But I was wrong.

The plate in front of me contained nothing that looked familiar to me. My face must have signaled something to my host.

Sitting beside me, he pointed to what looked like tiny rice grains. "Couscous, Wynne. A North African semolina product. On top, yams and garbanzos in a mild sauce. And this is a hot-pepper sauce to be used with caution." He passed me a tiny brass bowl with reverence. I took a small taste.

"This is delightful, Michael." He beamed. I was so relieved to be eating something that tasted good and that was of sufficient quantity that my mood lifted and I drained my glass.

After several more glasses and a second helping we walked arm in arm to the auction softly singing "Summertime." No cotton or corn grew in Juneau, but the summer living was certainly easier than the winter.

✳   ✳   ✳

A man in a cowboy hat stood on a dais at one end of the ballroom holding a landscape. I saw an arm waving. Royal pointed at the two seats beside him. He and Michael grinned at each other and Royal raised his eyebrows at me. "You've missed nothing. The auctioneer is starting with some boring pieces."

The bidding crawled. The man in the cowboy hat strode from one end of the dais to the other, pointing into the crowd. Finally the piece sold and he held up another painting, this one of several Tlingits in traditional dress standing in front of a longhouse flanked by two carved house posts. The bidding picked up and the final price reached the decent stage. Michael made notes as each painting came on the block.

"What on earth can you write about, Michael? What is interesting about an art auction?"

"The response, Wynne. Only people who buy art in Juneau came tonight. I'm going to do a piece for *Pacific Northwest* magazine on the effect of auctions on the market."

"Seems too esoteric to me."

Michael peered at the next painting. The auctioneer was pointing to the subject, an Indian woman cutting salmon in a fish camp. Broad flat strokes of color emphasized her prominent cheekbones and large brown eyes.

Michael bent over his notebook. "The bidding will be brisk for this one."

Royal leaned forward as the price was announced. "As long as the whites romanticize the Natives, that kind of piece will sell."

Michael nodded. "It's got to be life in the past, though. Living close to nature and all of that cow pattie." He checked his catalogue. "Watch this one, Royal. Even though it's not particularly well done, the price will go through the roof."

The chubby faces of two Indian girls in deerskin dresses, each holding a puppy, brought the bidding to a frenzied level. The artist, a white woman, sat a few rows away. Her face lit up at the final price. Michael and Royal looked at each and nodded. From then on they placed bets on the final price of each piece. It looked to me as if all they did was pass the same dollar back and forth. The paintings of Natives in traditional settings and clothing commanded the highest prices, watery landscapes placed second, and everything else including the abstract pieces trailed way behind in third.

After a struggle to sell one of those abstruse paintings that has everyone squinting, the auctioneer turned with relief to a large oil of Tlingit dancers in full regalia, obviously meant to evoke the soothing past. The bidding took off again. As the rather stiff final price was announced, Michael bolted upright from his slouched position. "Good God! of course!" He turned to me. "I've got to go!"

"Wait, Michael. What's the problem?"

Just then the overhead lights were turned up and the audience moved toward the lobby. We stood up and moved, victims of group think, with everyone else. Human beings can't help but do what everyone else is doing. Although the three of us were silent, excited little waves of people swirled and eddied around us. We were swept toward the bar, where we grabbed bottles of imported beer and crab-and-shrimp puffs from the banquet table. Moving away, we lifted the bottles as one, forming the still center of the whirlpool that circled around us. Alex Day and his frozen Nordic wife pointedly did not look at me. David and Greta surged toward the bar, throwing me a weak "hi" as they passed. Sonja strode through the crowd, draped with silver and turquoise Southwestern jewelry. She raised an ironic eyebrow at me. Ben Sinclair tipped a nonexistent hat in my direction, and Tyler drifted by, his eyes a little too bright. Voices rose and fell around us.

"I know who killed her, Royal."

The seriousness of Michael's pose frightened me. I don't know why. He turned to go after dropping his bombshell.

Royal touched his elbow. "Michael, don't leave us hanging. Who killed my cousin?"

"I don't want to say anything more until I've talked to Rita. I feel like an actor in a fifth-rate detective story. But I know now why they never tell anyone at first. They don't want to be laughed out of the script. Let me check my theory with Rita first."

I couldn't let him go alone. He wore a ridiculous tie, a silk silver salmon, and he looked vulnerable. "I'll go with you."

He waved a hand. "No, you two stay. I'll meet you for a drink after and tell you all about it. I know the Lone Ranger style is melodramatic, but I want to go alone."

Royal and I drained another bottle of Dos Equis quickly. It didn't even taste that good. When the chandeliers flickered, we veered toward the bathrooms before returning to our seats. I got back to mine first. Royal slipped into *his* seat after the auctioning started again, explaining that the lines were long in the men's room.

An hour later, when the last painting found a new home, Royal and I looked in the lobby and bar and restaurant for Michael. The search unsuccessful, we settled into the club chairs in the bar to wait, with small snifters of mediocre brandy.

Staring into the amber liquid, I jumped in with both feet. "I wish you had an alibi for the time your cousin was killed."

Royal's eyes widened. "You mean *I'm* an honest-to-God suspect? I . . . I don't know what to say."

I nodded. I wondered if a good detective tells people they are suspects.

Royal leaned forward. "Do you think that's why Michael wouldn't tell us who he suspected? Because he suspects *me?*" He sank back, talking to himself. "No, I can't believe it. Michael would have told me."

We didn't say much after that. The waiting dragged on and became an activity in itself. Every five minutes or so, one of us made the rounds in the hotel, in case Michael was looking for us.

Another hour passed. "I can't stand this, Royal. I'm calling Rita."

She was at home. Her voice had a distant quality. "Michael was coming to see me? About Magdalena?" She paused and I heard her hand cover the mouthpiece. Then she said, "Stay where you are, Wynne."

❉   ❉   ❉

We were staring into our brandy snifters when a dark-haired police officer I didn't recognize showed up. "Ma'am, Detective Manzoni would like to see you if it's convenient." He looked uncomfortable about not including Royal in the summons and couldn't meet his eyes.

"Call me tomorrow, Wynne." Royal touched my shoulder with the lightness of a bird's wing, and left.

The officer dropped me off without saying anything. The oil lantern glowed in the bay window. I trudged up the wooden steps, wondering if Michael was there too.

Rita led me to the round table and handed me a cup of hot herbal tea. "I'm afraid I have bad news for you, Wynne. Michael is in the hospital."

The apathy surrounding me lifted. "What?" My voice sounded too loud in the house.

She patted my hand. "We found him in a narrow space between two buildings, unconscious, about two hours ago. The doctors said we must have gotten to him shortly after he'd been hit."

"Hit?"

"On the head. He was a block up from the Baranof. Someone hit him on the head, hard enough to knock him out, and then dragged him a few feet off the sidewalk. The officers on the beat always make a practice of shining a flashlight into the alleys because the drunks huddle there."

"Is he going to survive?"

"Oh, yes. The doctors say he has a tough skull. They don't even think he would have died had he spent the night in the alley, but who knows?" She shrugged. "If it were winter instead of summer, his chances of surviving a blow and exposure would be much less." Rita poured some more tea out of a teapot with overblown roses on it. "I don't think whoever hit him wanted to kill him. Or maybe whoever hit him was interrupted. But my gut feeling is that this was a warning of some kind."

I described his cryptic message to Rita. "One minute we were watching them auction off paintings and the next minute he knows who the murderer is."

"Did he tell you?"

"He wouldn't tell us with all of those people milling around." All of those people . . . He'd told us he knew who the murderer was in front of half of Juneau.

"Who is 'us'?"

"Royal and me." Oh, dear. Why couldn't Royal have been somewhere far away?

"Try to remember who else you saw."

"Alex and Inga snubbed me, David and Greta swept by along with Ben and Sonja and Tyler and about three hundred other people."

Rita shifted in her chair. "Someone hit him five minutes after he left you, Wynne. Can you remember seeing those people after he left?"

My mind still felt numb. "I really can't remember, Rita. The lights went on and off right about then and we all returned to our seats." Lord! Royal hadn't. But I couldn't tell her that.

"I can see by your face that you've remembered something, Wynne."

The old hackneyed moment of truth arrived. Listening to the gently pattering rain on the windows, I spilled the information about Royal and felt disloyal.

Rita patted my hand again. "I know it's hard. But we are not after an innocent person. Do you want to stay here tonight? I can make up the couch."

No, I wanted to be in my own bed in my own house, listening to the rain on my roof. I knew I wouldn't be able to sleep and I called Royal as soon as I walked through the door to tell him about Michael. He wanted us to visit Michael in the morning.

"I don't know if we can, Royal. They have a guard posted and he is still unconscious."

Morning brought a need to talk to *someone*. I dressed quickly after a shower, grabbed a box off my kitchen shelf, and headed for Jane's. At six, it might as well have been ten for all of the light, but today a mist grayed the sky and blurred the outlines. I knew Jane would be on a mat in the living room stretching her way through her daily yoga ritual. She looked surprised when I arrived but waved me toward the kitchen. Making as little noise as possible, I added eggs to the boxed muffin mix and slipped them into the oven. I know her kitchen well and moved around with ease. White walls, white ceilings, white counters, white cabinets, and a white-tiled floor. And it was always spotless. A pegboard draped with pots and pans provided some color, as did the fire-engine-red tea kettle and tall stool. I cut up fruit from the basket on the counter and whisked herbs into some eggs. The coffee dripped through her Krupps and I was drinking some out of a shiny red mug when she came in looking relaxed and happy in a Swedish blue jumpsuit.

We sat in a small window alcove at a round table covered with a crisp square cloth. She pulled back the white lace café curtains and we breakfasted companionably, looking out at Mt. Roberts. The mist thinned and the sharp spruce outlines pricked the silver sky.

"I don't know what to think, Jane. It looks as if someone overheard Michael say that he knew who killed Magdalena. And then followed him out the door and hit him hard on the head, but not hard enough to kill him. That is what is puzzling to me. Why not kill him if you mean to protect yourself?"

Jane sipped her coffee. "Maybe it was intended as a warning. Or maybe the person wanted to kill him but couldn't at the last moment. Maybe it is someone who likes Michael." Jane didn't look at me as she said this.

I chose to ignore her oblique reference to Royal. "Or maybe whoever did it was desperate, not really thinking." I bit into the muffin. Blueberries spurted. "As an act of violence, it wasn't premeditated, was it? After all, the person who followed him out must have done it on the spur of the moment, right after hearing him say he knew who killed Magdalena."

"No, there really wasn't time to plan." Jane sounded pensive. "Why would the person believe Michael anyway? If *I* were the murderer, I would be very cautious. I would try to find out what someone knew but I wouldn't act."

"The murderer didn't have any time to be cautious, Jane. Michael announced that he was going to see Rita. He announced in a crowded room with all of the people involved within hearing distance that he was going to the police with vital information about a murder. I can see now how very dangerous that was."

Jane poured more coffee for us. "Let's call the hospital and find out if he can receive visitors yet."

Smiling as she returned to the kitchen, Jane gave me a thumbs-up. "They say he is resting comfortably and that he may receive some visitors. I imagine a police officer is screening visitors."

"I'm on my way. Cancel my first appointment, will you?"

My Volkswagen bug started immediately even though I hadn't used it for over a week. As I drove the four miles to the hospital, I felt so happy that Michael was not dead that I didn't even think once about Magdalena. Michael was sitting up with a blue and white hospital gown tied on backward and a white turban of bandages on his head. In his hand was the control for the television. He handed it to me. "Will you find Channel Twelve, Wynne? There's a soap opera on that I've always wanted to see, and I can't figure out these controls." He leaned back on his pillows with a satisfied sigh when I found the program. "This is the life, Wynne. Hand me the juice there, please." He sipped, eyes focused on the set. "A friend of mine used to watch this. He was a writer and got hooked on it. He rationalized by saying he planned to submit a script to them someday. I felt sorry for him, having to preserve his image by telling a transparent lie. Look at that!" He pointed up at the screen that hung above us. "A love scene and it's not even nine o'clock in the morning. Oh, Wynne, if you're not sick, hospitals can be fun."

"Michael, how is your head?"

"A little sore, but not bad. They're giving me something for the pain." He grinned. "I like that too. They're legal and make me feel sooooo good."

I wasn't about to be sidetracked into a discussion on drugs and their relative merits, legal or not. "Did you see who hit you?"

He shook his head, once again engrossed in the soap opera.

"Michael!" I wanted to shake him, but it probably wouldn't help anyway. "Who killed Magdalena?"

"I talked to Rita already this morning and she is going after the evidence now."

"Tell me who did it, Michael, before I shake you so hard your bandages fall off."

"Watch those lines in your forehead, Wynne. They're the first to show. Keep your face relaxed. See, look at that woman on the screen. Not a line showing, and she must be your age. The trick is prevention, Wynne." He settled back into his pillows.

"I give up, Michael. That blow to your head must have addled your brain."

"I'd like to tell you, Wynne, but Rita made me promise not to say a word. She told me to tell you to go to Tyler's show tomorrow night. I'll try to make it myself."

"Dreamer!" I scoffed as I headed out the door.

CHAPTER 10

By Sunday the weather changed with a sudden familiar intensity. The storm blew from the southeast, scooping up water in the channel, pushing clouds in front of it, making the wind sing. It was a perfect evening for thinking about myths and legends, the theme of Tyler's show. Even though it wouldn't be dark for hours, the rain clouds cast a gray light and sheets of mist skidded up the mountain only to evaporate into the storm at the top. Parka-clad walkers, identities hidden by hoods, scurried from awning to awning in brown knee-high rubber boots.

I hung up my rain gear in the gallery hall and slipped on a pair of pumps. The jackets and hats and boots stretched twenty feet. The place must be jammed. At the beginning of every show, serious buyers stake out their claims by standing beside the work, and Tyler, like a bee in lupin, buzzes from one to another, leaving red dots in his wake. My timing was perfect. I could see that the initial frenzy was over. No tight-jawed art lovers guarded the pieces. The only frantic person was Tyler, who swooped toward me with glittering eyes.

He grabbed my hands. "Lord, Wynne, what a rush. They bought almost everything and now they're running me out of champagne. I am ecstatic."

"You've worked hard for this moment, Tyler."

"Yes, but David is still holding out on me. Now he's using Magdalena's death as an excuse . . . but you must see the piece he did for this show. It is splendid." He kissed the tips of his fingers in an Italian gesture, unusually flamboyant for him, and tripped away.

Before I could get to the champagne, my eye was caught by a mask on the far wall. Examining it at closer range, I saw that the eyes were round and the mouth open. Reddish-brown in color, it resembled clay and, according to the label, depicted Land Otter Woman. I'm not familiar with all of the Tlingit myths, but many of them revolve around the mutative abilities of humans and animals, thus teaching about the close relationships among living things. Humans change into bears or salmon and have children who are both human and animal. I suppose that theme is one that resonates in all cultures. Look at the Minotaur in Greek mythology. Masks are disturbing to me, and this one was no exception. How a shell with a face can be so powerful eludes me. A voice at my shoulder broke into my reverie.

"It's made of cedar bark."

"I don't believe it." I responded automatically without

turning around. Then I registered the voice that had triggered the familiar warmth in my stomach. "Oh, since it's you," I said, turning around, "I suppose I should believe it."

Royal smiled. "I have it on good authority—from the artist herself. Cecelia gathered the bark, made it into paper, and molded it into the mask you see before you."

"She must be Tlingit to have found the cedar."

"You are right, Wynne. The Tlingits have managed to keep the location of the cedar trees a secret for many years. I think it's a holdover from the time we used them for canoes. Now we just like to keep secrets."

"Did Magdalena have a secret?"

His face actually lengthened in sorrow. "I think she had several." Tears glistened in his eyes. "What a waste. Well, it's almost over now."

"What do you mean?" For one painful moment I thought he was going to confess.

Instead of answering, he took my hand, tucked it into his arm, and led me through the arched doorway into the little room where the champagne was. On the long table an enormous bouquet of orange tiger lilies spilled out of a crystal vase. We stood looking out the window at the channel where the whitecaps were visible. Royal turned to me with a sudden intensity, leaning forward in a conspiratorial way. "Do you know what a totem pole is?"

My first reaction, unspoken, was that, of course, I know what a totem pole is. In Juneau we have perhaps twenty of them scattered about. I see them every day. Yet, I really don't see them in the sense that they hold little meaning for me. They are monumental sculptures that beautify the landscape. Period. "No, I don't know what a totem pole is."

He picked up an almost full bottle of champagne and two glasses and we walked to a small table next to the window. He poured us each a glass. "As you know, the Tlingit language has only recently been written, long after most Tlingits have assimilated into the white culture." He sipped his champagne. "Long ago, the Tlingits passed on their culture in drama and dance and storytelling and in their art. They made beautiful objects, Wynne. Spoons, bowls, boxes, blankets, baskets, screens, and, of course, totem poles."

"Totem poles are a way of passing on the Tlingit culture?"

"In a way, yes, they are. The Tlingits had a special relationship with the earth and the animals. Totem poles express that. All animals possess spirits and powers that we identify with. Every family identifies with a certain animal almost as a crest, or, as Europeans might conceive of it, our coat of arms."

"You mean that totem poles describe someone's lineage?"

"Yes and no. I'm afraid it isn't that simple."

It never is, I thought to myself. The totem poles, for me, had just blended into the general landscape. I enjoy them for their strong shapes and colors, but I have never troubled to find out the stories connected with them. They were symbols of another culture, as meaningless to me as medieval paintings of Jesus and Mary must be to Hindus.

Royal waited for me to finish my thoughts before he spoke again. Extremely sensitive man! "Heraldic or memorial poles are probably the most common. In fact, in old photographs of villages, totem poles were as common as telephone poles are today. I'm afraid that relatively few remain." He stopped then, perhaps thinking of the invasion of European and American culture that snowballed around the turn of the century and obliterated much of the Tlingit culture and which even now threatens the very lives of the young Natives who are caught in between. "So many were lost to the rainy climate and people's ignorance of their value." He sighed, then, as a scholar who feels the full impact of something priceless lost forever. "I've strayed from my lecture. I don't know if it is the Tlingit or the scholar in me who wants to make this presentation more elaborate."

He could have talked all night, for all I cared. Not only was he gorgeous, but he moved beautifully too.

I could only nod, my mouth having gone dry. He hadn't affected me like this the night we waited for Michael. I felt fourteen again.

He ticked off on his fingers as he listed. "Besides the heraldic poles, there are grave figures, house posts, housefront poles, welcoming poles, and mortuary poles. All have different meanings, and are used for different purposes. They all feature sculptures of humans and animals on top on one another in a certain order. There are even several Abraham Lincoln poles, realistic renderings of him in a top hat probably made at the time he was assassinated. All of them can be interpreted if one knows the symbols, the mythology, and the history of the clan as well as their social customs."

"It is fascinating, Royal, but I am in the dark about why we are talking about totem poles now."

Royal looked surprised and then chuckled, shaking his

head. "It's *not* just an excuse for me to show off. Come, let me show you something."

We made our way through the still large crowd to stand before an enormous canvas I must have been blind to miss when I'd walked in.

Royal pointed to it. "David did this and it puzzles me."

I peered at it. The composition was unusual. It was not a front view of a totem pole, but one that captured part of the front and part of the side so that the detail on the side assumed the center of the painting. Tilted toward a Sitka spruce, the chipped and worn paint of green-blue and black and red-orange almost blended into the rain forest. At the top perched a raven, and underneath a salmon whose tail curved around the side of the pole, riveting the eye. It was spread like a fan, and drops of rain glistened on it. Farther down on the pole was a bear and a beaver. But the eye kept returning to the salmon tail. It was so evocative of something, I don't know what. The title on the little white card next to it was also evocative: "Alaskan Family Tree."

"I love it," I whispered to Royal.

"Me too," he whispered back. And in his normal voice he added, "And I want to get to the bottom of this. Come along."

Bottom of what? He took my elbow and we approached David, almost as if we were stalking him. David, waist cinched in a satin jacket, smiled at us as we came up. Greta was with David and nodded to me mechanically.

Royal pointed to the painting. "I like it very much, David."

David assumed his "aw, shucks" pose. "Thank you, Royal, that means a lot to me."

"I haven't seen that totem pole around town. Where did you find it?"

David's head came up and his eyelids covered half his eyes. "You wouldn't have seen it, Royal. It doesn't exist. Except in my imagination."

"That surprises me. I don't think I've ever seen a painting of an imaginary totem pole. I know that most painters, sometime in their careers, take a crack at doing a totem pole, but they choose real ones."

David waved his hand as though the rest were sterile fools who had to rely on reality while the real artist could create his own totem pole. "I never found one I wanted to paint."

"What about the title? I don't understand it."

"All the animals are Alaskan, part of the wildlife family here." He spread his hands as if to say "there, now wasn't that simple?"

Royal nodded sagaciously and moved away, me being pulled along in his wake. Then Rita came in the room, looking radiant in a black silk dress trimmed with lace at the collar and cuffs. When he saw her, Royal almost ran to her. What I heard him whisper to her, there in Tyler's gallery, stunned me. She nodded twice, her face immobile, and said, "It makes sense, Royal. He couldn't have done that painting even if he *had* seen the pole. It is too cerebral and moving. He has neither the skill nor the intelligence. Anyone can see he is shallow and lacks insight. His earlier work—picture-postcard animals—is the highest level *he* can ever attain."

I thrust myself forward. "Then who painted all of the pieces that catapulted him into the international limelight?"

They turned to me and spoke as one. "Magdalena."

My stomach lurched as I watched Rita stroll over to David, who was standing by himself. I followed, eager to hear what was being said. "David," she said softly. "I know you've been signing your name to Magdalena's paintings."

"You must be crazy." He looked around wildly to see if anyone was listening. I don't think he saw me. I don't know that he really saw anyone, though Greta suddenly appeared at his side, protective.

Rita shook her head, smiling slightly at the futility of David's denial. "You couldn't get away with it for long, David. Someone was bound to find out."

David's face was strained. "There is nothing to find out, Rita." He lifted his head and turned to Greta as if to take her arm and leave, when Rita spoke again.

"This painting is your downfall, David. You tried to pass it off as a creation of your imagination. But it is *real*. It exists, David. In Ka'saan, a place you have never been. It is a very well-known pole because it is the only one in the world that has a salmon on it. It is even called the Salmon Pole by those who prize its uniqueness. Magdalena painted it from memory."

David suddenly shouted, "Magdalena wasn't a painter!"

Rita straightened her broad shoulders. People, alerted by the shout, edged closer. "That painting, and all of the others like it, the totemic work, is Magdalena's. Not yours."

David swung his head from side to side, eyes down, voice low. "You don't know what you're talking about!"

Rita was relentless. "She tricked you, David. She was fed up with you getting all of the credit. She knew someone would recognize this pole and challenge your ridiculous assertion that you 'created it.' It isn't an Alaskan animal family tree at all. It is an Alaskan Family Tree—Magdalena's. It is a visual history of her family. That's why she gave it that title."

David's face grew slack. He looked around dully at the people who were listening. "I never thought she would do something like that to me."

Rita moved closer and spoke, almost lovingly. "And all your hopes and dreams about your work started turning to ashes."

David's body curved into the shape of an infant, sagging and slumping. "I didn't *mean* to kill her. But she was going to tell."

I met Royal and Rita at Lucille's for breakfast the next morning. When I arrived, they were discussing visual art.

Rita moved along the red-padded booth to make room for me. "Wynne, I'm going to fill my walls. This case has given me something positive—a beginning appreciation of fine art. I started my collection last night."

"With what? Not Magdalena's painting?"

"No, that will go to her family. I couldn't afford it anyway. I bought the mask of the 'Land Otter Woman.'"

Lucille appeared, laden with thick white platters of delicately flavored hash browns, thin slices of bone-in Virginia ham, and a large bowl of cut-up fresh fruit. In the center of the table she set down a large thermos of hot coffee. She grinned at us as she left.

"I *still* can't believe that Magdalena was a painter."

Royal looked up from his plate. "I feel much better about her death now. I was haunted by a sense of having let her down, that I should have steered her in the right direction somehow. But now I realize that she was steering *herself* in the right direction. She was doing what she wanted to do and she was doing it so well." He stopped, his voice breaking a little.

Rita patted Royal's arm. "We searched his place after we arrested him and found a diary hidden by Magdalena that documented her secret life as an artist. Apparently when she started painting he convinced her that exhibiting under his name would guarantee that they would sell. I think she was also very hesitant about exposing herself to the public eye. As she grew in confidence, realizing that her work was good, she became dissatisfied. Somehow he kept her from telling until that night at the party, when he joined in with the other men in putting down female artists. She must have decided then to come out as an artist herself. Naturally her doing so would expose him as a fake."

I was still puzzled by one thing. "But how did Michael know that David was a fake? He hadn't even seen the Alaskan Family Tree."

Rita lit a cigarette. "Actually, the light bulb flashed after a conversation you had with Michael about an artist's soul."

Friday night's African dinner seemed so long ago. "He did spout some nonsense about being able to identify a personal philosophy by studying an artist's work."

Royal raised an ironic eyebrow. "Wynne, feelings are your métier and art appreciation your avocation. I'm surprised you don't agree with him."

I had to think for a moment about that. "Perhaps my appreciation is of a different sort. It is the work that speaks to me, not the person who created it. I guess that I never connect the two."

Rita leaned forward. "Well, it is Michael's business to do just that. When I saw him in the hospital, he told me that he had an insight at the auction when he realized that the sentimental renditions of Native life were all painted by whites. And that David's paintings all portrayed the reality of living in two very dissimilar cultures. And that a person could not do that without personal experience, not even a person of great sensitivity."

"So he knew that someone else must have painted them, and it had to be Magdalena."

They both nodded.

Now that I knew more about her I felt a keener loss. "What a terrible waste. And I don't think I ever suspected him. I guess I should stick to my practice and forget about detecting, Rita."

Royal took my hand as Rita spoke. "I couldn't have done it without your insights, Wynne. Don't turn in your badge yet. I might need you again sometime."